PONY CLUB
SECRETS

Storm and the
Silver Bridle

The Pony Club Secrets series:

Also available in the series:

Coming Soon...

PONY CLUB SECRETS

Storm and the Silver Bridle

STACY GREGG

HarperCollins *Children's Books*

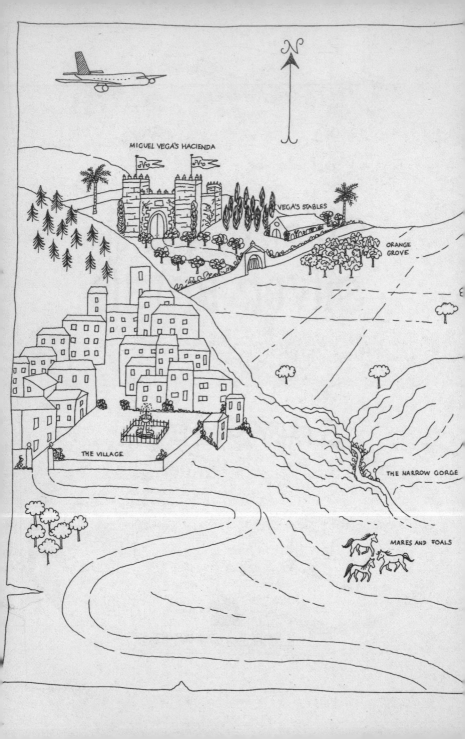

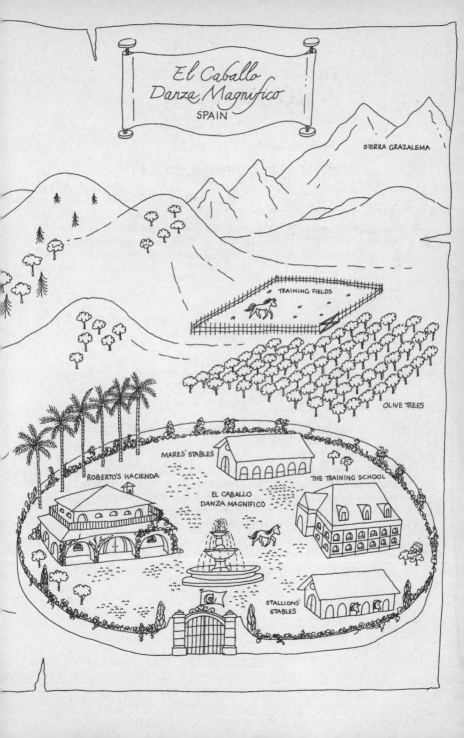

For my dad, thanks for
buying me a pony

www.stacygregg.co.uk

First published in Great Britain by HarperCollins *Children's Books* in 2009.
HarperCollins *Children's Books* is a division of HarperCollins*Publishers* Ltd,
77-85 Fulham Palace Road, Hammersmith, London, W6 8JB.

5

Text copyright © Stacy Gregg 2009
Illustrations © Fiona Land 2009

ISBN-13 978-0-00-727031-6

The author and illustrator assert the moral right to be identified
as the author and illustrator of the work.

Printed and bound in England by Clays Ltd, St Ives plc

Mixed Sources
Product group from well-managed
forests and other controlled sources
www.fsc.org Cert no. SW-COC-1806
© 1996 Forest Stewardship Council

FSC is a non-profit international organisation established to promote the
responsible management of the world's forests. Products carrying the FSC
label are independently certified to assure consumers that they come
from forests that are managed to meet the social, economic and
ecological needs of present and future generations.

Find out more about HarperCollins and the environment at
www.harpercollins.co.uk/green

Chapter 1

Anyone who knows anything about horses will tell you that there is no such thing as a white horse. A horse is never called 'white'. They are always referred to as grey.

Roberto Nunez shook his head and smiled at this. How silly these rules were!

He knew that horses could not be white. Yet how else could he describe the mares that were galloping towards him? These mares were as pure white as the snow that topped the distant mountains of the Sierra de Grazalema. They were as white as the stone walls that ran around the stables here at El Caballo Danza Magnifico.

Roberto Nunez's purebred Lipizzaner mares were as white as any animal in nature could possibly be. Their colour appeared all the more startling because it was in stark contrast with the coal-black foals that ran alongside them at their feet.

Although Lipizzaner horses are famous for being white, their foals are always born pitch-black. Gradually, as the foals grow up, their colour will change. As they mature, the Lipizzaners' dark coat will begin to prick here and there with tiny white hairs so that by the time the foals have grown into yearlings they have become steel-grey. At the age of three Lipizzaners are almost grown-up, and their coats have become even lighter, with dapples beginning to show through the dark steel on their hindquarters. In this way, their coats will keep fading until finally, at around the age of twelve, their dapples will have washed away and the Lipizzaner will be utterly and completely snow-white just like their mothers and fathers before them.

This was the way with the Lipizzaner. Roberto Nunez knew the breed well. At his *hacienda*, his grand estate here in southern Spain, he bred Andalusians and Lipizzaners, along with the highly strung, elegant, chestnut Anglo-Arabs that made up his internationally renowned troupe of performing horses known as El Caballo Danza Magnifico.

The mares that were galloping towards him now, driven carefully by his men, were part of his breeding herd. They had been grazing for the day out on the dry, rocky hillsides that surrounded his horse stud. Nunez liked to let the mares and their young foals roam free as much as possible. It toughened them up. It gave them spirit. But always he kept a close eye on his horses. Now, as night fell, he was bringing them home.

There were about two dozen mares in this herd, all ghostly pale, with the bloom of their grey dapples fading on their rumps. Their manes and tails were hogged off – cropped short, in the style that the Spanish always kept their breeding herds. It was funny, Nunez thought, how his mares were the ones who had their hair cropped short while the stallions, the male horses of the herd, were allowed to keep their long and silky manes.

Even without their manes, these mares were great beauties. To anyone else, they would have appeared almost identical, and yet Nunez could tell them apart at a glance. He simply looked at their faces and knew them instantly, in the same way that you and I might know a friend's face if we saw her in a crowded street.

For instance, one mare might have a Roman nose, a noble trait often seen in the Lipizzaner, while another mare would possess the dished face of the Arabian bloodlines that had also influenced this mighty breed. Some mares had the typical Lipizzaner characteristic of perfect almond-shaped eyes. Others were blessed with a smattering of the dainty freckles known as 'flea-bites' flecked on their cheeks.

These were Roberto Nunez's very best mares and they had been bred with the very best of El Caballo Danza Magnifico's stallions.

Roberto Nunez smiled now as he caught sight of one of his favourite mares, Margarita, with her pretty coal-dark eyes and her features so delicate she looked as if she might have been carved out of marble. At Margarita's feet was a jet-black foal. The foal was all legs, gangly and awkward, and only a few weeks old. And yet already Roberto Nunez could see the signs of greatness in him that came from being sired by one of the finest stallions in Spain.

"You see him, Marius?" Nunez said to the stallion beneath him. The great grey horse shifted about restlessly at the sound of his master's voice, and Nunez reached down and gave him a firm pat on his arched, glossy neck. "That is your son," he said proudly.

The progeny of Marius held the key to the future of El Caballo Danza Magnifico. Roberto Nunez knew it. And this foal was not the only one. He had discovered that there was another son of his mighty stallion, born far away from Spain – in New Zealand, of all places!

His head instructor, Francoise D'arth, had received a letter from a girl called Isadora Brown. The letter said that a foal had been born to her mare Blaze and that Marius was the father! Nunez could not believe it when he heard the news. But one look at the photos of the colt that the girl enclosed removed any doubts. He was clearly the progeny of Marius, as strong and handsome as his famous sire. And with the beautiful Anglo-Arab mare Blaze as his dam, the colt would be intelligent too.

The colt's name was Nightstorm – although in her letter the girl referred to him by his nickname. She called him Storm.

The thunder of hooves shook Roberto Nunez back to reality as the mares and foals rushed past just in front of him, heading in through the wrought-iron gates that led into the vast courtyard of El Caballo stables. As the herd ran past, Nunez searched again for Margarita and her foal and then laughed out loud as he caught a glimpse of the black colt in full flight, giving a high-spirited buck as he raced through the gates.

"You see, Marius?" Nunez murmured to the stallion. "Your son. He is coming home..."

Meanwhile, on the other side of the world, Issie Brown was having serious second thoughts about taking Storm away from Winterflood Farm.

"I don't know about this, Tom," she said, gazing uncertainly at her colt standing in his stall. "Are you sure he's ready?"

"Absolutely," Tom Avery said. "The journey will be no big deal. This is an important stage in his training."

"It's just that he's still so little." Issie's voice was quivering. "He's only just been weaned two weeks ago and he's never been away from the farm before—"

"Issie, he'll be fine," Avery said firmly.

"But Tom—"

"Honestly, Isadora!" Avery couldn't keep the exasperation out of his voice. "With the fuss you're making you'd swear we were taking Storm halfway around the world instead of ten minutes down the road. For Pete's sake! We're only driving to the pony club grounds! It's hardly a long trip, is it? Trust me, he's ready!"

Issie sighed. "You're right, Tom. I'm being silly."

She had to face the fact that Storm wasn't her baby any more. The colt was so grown-up he was already as tall as his dam, Blaze. He shared his mother's delicate Anglo-Arabian features too, although his big-boned, powerful physique and presence owed more to his sire, Marius.

Storm was six months old now. Had it really been that long since the stormy night when the foal was born? Issie remembered it so clearly, fighting the rain to get Blaze inside, sheltering in the stable as the lightning flashes lit up the pitch-black sky. The thunderstorm that had marked the colt's sudden arrival into the world had given him his name – Nightstorm. Issie had delivered him all by herself, and from the moment she saw the wee foal lying damp and newborn on the straw of the stable floor she had fallen in love with him.

The only living creature that loved Storm as much as Issie did was the foal's mother, Blaze. They were so alike, Blaze and her son. Even though Storm was a bay and his mother was a chestnut, the colt's broad white blaze that ran down his velvety nose made him look just like his mum. He was beautiful like her too, with those enormous eyes full of wonder, fringed with eyelashes that were so long they didn't even look real.

With his fluffy dark mane and doe eyes, Storm was as cute as a baby kitten. If Issie had been left to her own devices, she would have spoilt him rotten with cuddles and treats. But Avery knew better than to let her do that. Her pony-club instructor had made it clear right from the start that horses weren't pets to be mollycoddled and fussed over.

"That foal is going to grow into a big, strong horse one day, bigger and stronger than you are," he told her firmly. "So don't even think about teaching it some tricks that you might think are cute right now, but will turn dangerous later on when that colt gets older. You are training a horse to respect you right from the start."

Issie was beyond grateful when Avery offered to keep Storm at Winterflood Farm and help her with his training. Together they began to 'imprint' the foal, teaching Storm to wear a halter, to lead and to stand politely while they brushed him and picked up his hooves.

Still, there were some things that Issie simply couldn't bring herself to do. When the colt was five months old and Avery decided that he was ready for weaning, Issie knew she couldn't bear to watch Storm and Blaze be separated.

"Can you do it, Tom?" she said, with tears welling in her eyes. "I don't think I'll be able to stand it. It's better if I just stay home."

Avery understood. "It's a normal process for all mares and foals to be split up, but they'll be upset for a day or so," he said. "I think it would be best to keep Storm here at Winterflood Farm in familiar surroundings.

He'll feel more secure if he's in his usual field. I'll take Blaze down to the River Paddock."

And so on the day of the weaning Issie sat at home hugging her knees miserably and watching bad movies on TV, while Avery separated the mare and her foal for the first time.

Blaze had been frantic when she was taken away from her son. She had whinnied and whinnied and paced up and down the fenceline, with a heartbreaking expression on her face as she searched in vain for her baby. But eventually she calmed down and began to graze and make friends again with her old paddock mates Toby and Coco.

As for Storm, the little colt had bellowed for his mother solidly all day and into the night. Then, just before Avery went to bed, he heard the trip-trap of the colt's hooves on the gravel driveway. Storm had decided that no one was keeping him away from his mum any longer and had jumped out of his paddock!

Issie couldn't believe it when Avery called to tell her. "Well, on the positive side, at least we know now that he has the makings of a good showjumper," Avery said. Luckily the driveway gate had been shut and Avery had caught the colt before he got too far. "Don't worry," he told Issie, "I've put him back in the magnolia paddock this time where the fences are a metre higher. I doubt he'll get out again."

With his attempted jailbreak foiled, Storm seemed to resign himself to his fate and began to make friends with Avery's two horses, Starlight and Vinnie, who grazed in the paddock next to his. By the time Issie arrived at Winterflood Farm the next day she found her colt quite content with his new life without his mum, nickering happily over the fence to her.

"It's all part of growing up," Avery told her. "He's becoming a horse." Issie knew her instructor was right, but still, she worried about her colt.

Now Avery said Storm was ready for the next step – his first outing. For the past two weeks Issie had been practising with the colt in Avery's horse float. At first she had simply got Avery to park the float around the back of the house in Storm's paddock. She had dropped the ramp and let the colt sniff his way around it, putting one tentative hoof and then another onboard. Then, she had clipped a lead rope to his halter and led the colt all the way on and off the horse float, talking softly to him whenever he spooked or snorted, reassuring him that it was OK and nothing would hurt him.

By the end of the second week, Storm was so comfortable around the horse float that he would walk on all by himself and stand like a perfect gentleman as Issie fussed with his halter, tied up his hay net and then lifted the ramp and locked the colt safely inside. Once he was closed in she would leave him standing there for a few moments, just to let him see how it felt before she lowered the ramp and let him out again.

Today the routine would be just the same as the past couple of weeks, Issie told herself. Except today, instead of going nowhere and staying in the paddock, the horse float was attached to the towbar of Avery's Range Rover.

"Easy, Storm," Issie cooed to the colt. "We're just going to go for a little ride."

Storm lifted his legs in an exaggerated high step, wary of the leg bandages that Issie had put on him today to protect him for the journey. The colt raised his feet deliberately and precisely as he walked up the float ramp. Then he was inside and Issie was bolting the doors behind him before climbing into the Range Rover next to Avery.

"Is he ready?" Avery asked.

Issie took a deep breath and nodded. "Uh-huh. Let's go."

As the Range Rover rolled slowly down the driveway,

Issie twisted round in her seat and stared out of the back window at the float.

"Is he OK?" Avery asked her.

"He's fine, Tom." Issie turned to her instructor. "I guess I shouldn't have worried so much, but it's his first ride in the horse float, you know?"

Avery smiled at her. "The pony club is the perfect distance – just a few kilometres. That's a good first trip for him. It will get him used to travelling and being around other horses. It's all about breaking him in gradually to new experiences. We start him off by taking him to pony-club rally. Let him understand that it's not a big deal, just tether him to the float for an hour or so, let him look around, then bring him home again. By the time he goes out to compete at his first gymkhana or one-day event he'll be quite relaxed because he knows the drill."

Issie nodded. Then she turned back to stare out of the rear window again, keeping her eyes locked on the horse float to make sure Storm was still OK.

If she hadn't been so busy staring straight at the horse float she might have noticed the car that was trailing behind them to the pony-club grounds. It was a black sedan with tinted windows, and it had been following them ever since it pulled out from behind the trees next to Winterflood Farm.

The black car kept its distance, travelling slowly behind them all the way to the pony club. When Avery pulled up to open the gates of the Chevalier Point club grounds, the sedan pulled over and parked out of sight behind the hedge across the road. A tinted window was lowered and a pair of binoculars appeared. Through the binoculars, dark eyes were watching Issie and her colt. They watched as Storm came down the ramp of the float, the binoculars trained directly on the colt as he looked about excitedly, letting out a shrill whinny, calling to the other horses. They saw the way Issie held the colt's head firmly and talked to him all the time, and the way the colt responded to her voice, calming down as she handled him.

Then, satisfied that they had seen enough, the tinted window was rolled shut again and the black car silently drove off.

If only Issie had seen the car, she might have realised that there was something suspicious going on. But as the black sedan swept out of sight, she had no idea of the danger they were in. She did not know what was to come – for her, and for Nightstorm.

Chapter 2

Issie might not have noticed the black sedan, but it was hard to miss the sour-faced spectacle that greeted her as they pulled into the club grounds.

Natasha Tucker had spent pretty much the whole season at pony club trying to make Issie's life a misery. As Avery steered the truck through the gates and Issie caught sight of the girl with the stiff blonde plaits glowering malevolently at her it was clear that today was going to be no different.

Issie knew precisely why Stuck-up Tucker had her in her sights. Ever since the Horse of the Year Show, when Issie and her skewbald pony Comet had beaten Natasha, the girls had openly been at war. Natasha was still furious that Issie's aunt Hester had refused to sell Comet to her.

Natasha's trainer, Ginty McLintoch, had offered Hester a huge amount of money – $28,000! But Hester had turned her down and given the skewbald showjumper to Issie instead.

Natasha didn't take no for an answer. She always got what she wanted and, despite the fact that she kept telling Issie that skewbalds were ugly, she had decided she wanted Comet. Ginty McLintoch had approached Issie twice since then on Natasha's behalf and offered to buy the skewbald gelding. But each time Issie said no – which just infuriated Natasha even more.

Issie would never have given up Comet. She had really bonded with the skewbald since she brought him home to the pony club at the beginning of summer. Now summer was over – and so was pony club. The weather was turning rainy and miserable and the club grounds were already getting boggy. Today would be the last rally for a while. For the next month or so, during the very worst of the weather, the club would be closed and most of the Chevalier Point riders, including Issie, had decided to spell their horses over this time, leaving them unridden until conditions improved.

Issie had been torn when she realised that bringing Storm along today meant she would miss her chance to ride Comet at the final rally of the season. She had even thought she might be able to ride Blaze to pony club today for the first time in ages. After all, Storm had been weaned so the mare was able to be ridden again. But Avery had convinced her to leave Blaze and Comet at home. It was more important, he said, to use this opportunity to give Storm his first experience of the grown-up horsey world. This was a vital part of the colt's training, letting him get used to new sights and sounds, and other horses. Not that there was any point in trying to explain that to Natasha.

"So why are you bringing your foal to pony club? What's the point of that?" huffed Natasha as she strode over from her fancy blue and silver horse truck where she had been standing to watch Issie unload Storm. "Trying to show off, I suppose. You always have to be the centre of attention, don't you?"

"I am not showing off!" Issie was taken aback. "Coming here is part of Nightstorm's training. Avery says—"

"Avery says, Avery says…" Natasha sing-songed back. She cast a glance over her shoulder to make sure Avery was still inside the horse truck and couldn't hear her before she went on, "You know, some of us don't care what Avery has to say. He's just a pony-club instructor. If he was any good then he'd have his own private stables, wouldn't he?"

"Like Ginty McLintoch, I suppose?" Issie said archly. She was fed up with Natasha banging on about her fabulous, expensive lessons with Ginty, and complaining about Avery's 'dated methods'.

"Ginty McLintoch says she'd never teach at a pony club," Natasha said. "She says she's too professional to lower her standards—"

"Natasha!" There was a call from the blue and silver horse truck and Mrs Tucker appeared on the ramp, looking flustered. "Natasha! What's going on? Are you going to unload your horse or do I have to do everything?"

Natasha groaned out loud at her mother's command, but she did as she was asked and walked back over to her truck, following Mrs Tucker back inside. A few moments later she emerged again leading a horse. Issie had been expecting to see Natasha's elegant rose-grey, Fabergé. Instead, the horse that appeared was a striking chestnut, about sixteen hands high, with a glossy coat, perfectly pulled mane, flowing tail and two white hind socks.

"His name is Romeo and he's a purebred Selle Francaise – a French sport-horse!" Natasha said proudly as she led him past Issie and tied him up.

Issie was stunned. "What happened to Fabergé?"

"Fabby's gone," Natasha shrugged. "He was never talented enough for me. Ginty was supposed to find me a new horse at Horse of the Year, but really there was nothing there that measured up to my needs." Natasha said this last part with a nasty sneer and Issie knew this was a dig at Comet. "Anyway, that's when Mummy suggested that Ginty fly over to Australia and look for a new horse to bring back. That's where she found Romeo. She insists that Romeo is the perfect horse to take me to the national pony club champs, and—"

"Got a new horse then?" Stella interrupted as she rode up to join them. "Is that because Fabergé kept bucking you off?"

Natasha gave Stella a filthy look. "That wasn't my fault! Fabergé is too highly strung. Ginty says that's why we weren't clicking."

"Natasha, I don't know how you can expect to 'click' with a horse if you just keep getting new ones every time something goes wrong!" Stella shot back.

"It's called upgrading," Natasha sniffed. She cast her eyes over Coco. "You know, you should really think about upgrading too, Stella. You're so huge your legs are almost dragging on the ground on that pony. What's the matter? Can't your parents afford to buy you a new one?"

Stella seemed genuinely hurt by this and Natasha, pleased with the success of her put-down, decided that was the end of the conversation. "I'm glad this is the last rally of the year," she added icily as she turned to lead Romeo away to the washing bays. "That means I won't have to put up with you two again for the next few months."

"God, she is such a cow!" Stella said, pulling a face behind Natasha's back as she watched her walk away. Then she vaulted out of the saddle to stand beside her horse. "Never mind what Stuck-up Tucker says, Coco, I still love you!" Stella threw her arms around Coco's neck, giving the mare a snuggle. Coco, who didn't particularly like snuggles, put her ears back a bit.

"You are getting a bit big for her though, aren't you?" Issie said gently.

It was true. The girls were fourteen now and Stella had really grown this year. Coco was only thirteen-two hands high and Stella looked enormous on her. Her legs were so long they almost wrapped right around the mare's tubby brown belly.

"I know…" Stella said. She cast a sneaky sideways glance at Coco, as if she was checking to see if the pony was listening, and then whispered dramatically to Issie with her hand over her face. "I don't really want to talk about this in front of Coco, but I've been looking in the 'ponies for sale' pages in *PONY* magazine. Mum and Dad said that I can sell Coco and get a new pony in time for summer and they're taking me to look at this fourteen-two roan next week…"

"Stella," Issie whispered back, "you do know that you don't have to whisper, don't you? Coco can't understand English."

"Coco understands every word I say, don't you, Coco?" Stella giggled, stroking her mare's forelock.

While the girls were talking, Storm had been standing obediently tied up beside them, his head held high, watching everything that was going on around him with bright, wide eyes. Mostly though, he was looking intently at Coco. He gave a high-pitched whinny and stretched to the end of his lead rope, craning his neck to get closer to her.

"Hey, Storm!" Stella said. "Do you want to say hello to Coco?"

Issie nodded. "That's why we're here. Tom says it will be good for Storm to socialise with other horses."

At first, Storm stepped back nervously when Stella led Coco over. After a few moments, though, his curiosity got the better of him and he came closer, stretching his neck out so that he and Coco were touching noses. Coco responded with a stroppy squeal and put her ears flat back, trying to nip at the colt. Nightstorm skittered back to get out of her way.

"Coco! Be nice! He's just a baby," Stella scolded. She stood Coco still and waited for Nightstorm to try again. This time the mare reluctantly seemed to accept the colt's presence. They nickered to each other softly, as if they were making horsey conversation, and within a few minutes they were standing quite happily together.

"Where's Kate?" Issie wondered.

"She's waiting for the farrier," Stella said. "Toby threw a shoe."

"We have to get her to introduce Toby to Nightstorm too," Issie said. "Maybe the three of them will be best friends – just like us."

Issie, Stella and Kate had been inseparable from the moment they met. Issie's mum always said that the girls were so alike they must be sisters. This was kind of a joke, because the three of them didn't actually look anything like each other. Issie had olive skin and long, dark straight hair just like her mum. Stella was a redhead with curls and freckles and Kate was tall and lanky with short-bobbed blonde hair and pale blue eyes. "Never mind looks. On the inside, where it matters, you three girls are cut from the same cloth," Mrs Brown would say, smiling and shaking her head. "Utterly horse-mad!"

Issie looked at her watch. Quarter to nine. The rally was about to start and she was absolutely dying of thirst. She had just enough coins in her pocket to use the drinks machine in the clubroom.

"Stella," she said, "can you do me a favour? Can you watch Storm for a couple of minutes? I want to get a drink."

"I want one too. I'll come with you," Stella said.

Issie shook her head. "Tom said I shouldn't leave Storm alone by himself."

Stella looked at Storm, who was happily nibbling at his hay net. "He's not alone. He's with Coco," she said. "He'll be fine. We'll only be a minute."

"I know, but…" Issie wasn't sure about this, but she didn't want to be a drama queen. After all, they were only going to the clubroom.

"OK, OK!" she caved. "But we have to be quick, all right?"

The two girls raced across the paddock to the clubroom and bounded up the steps. Issie dug into her pockets and hastily fed the change into the drinks machine. She listened for the clunk-clunk, and then stuck her hand into the hole to retrieve her can of Coke.

"Ohhh, I might get some crisps too!" Stella said. "I love crisps for breakfast." She grinned at Issie as she put her money in the vending machine.

"Come on. We better get back," Issie said nervously. She was beginning to regret leaving Storm. Avery had been quite firm when he told her not to leave the colt tied up by himself. If anything happened she wouldn't forgive herself.

Issie stepped out of the clubroom and looked back towards the horse float where Storm was tethered. "Ohmygod!" she said.

"What's wrong?" Stella said. But Issie didn't answer her. She had already leapt off the clubroom steps and was sprinting back across the paddock.

Issie could feel her heart pounding in her chest as she ran towards the horse float. Storm was standing where she had left him – but there was a dark figure next to the colt, with one hand grasping Storm's halter.

"Hey!" Issie yelled as she ran across the paddock. "Hey!"

At the sound of Issie's voice, the dark figure turned round. It was a woman. She was dressed in crisp white jodhpurs, long black boots and a black shirt. Her face was hidden behind dark glasses and the dramatic sweep of her long dark hair, but that didn't matter. Issie had recognised her even before she caught a glimpse of her features.

"You came!" Issie's face broke into a broad grin as she ran towards the woman. "I hadn't heard anything for so long, I had almost given up!"

The woman, who had been gently stroking the colt's muzzle, whispered something to the young horse and let go of the halter. She stepped forward to greet Issie, giving her two brisk kisses, one on each cheek, just as the French always do, before wrapping her in her arms in the most enormous hug.

"Isadora!" the woman cried. "*Bonjour!* It is so good to see you once again!"

Issie couldn't believe it. It was Francoise D'arth. The famed French horsewoman, head rider of El Caballo Danza Magnifico, here at Chevalier Point!

The last time Francoise had arrived in Chevalier Point with her troupe of dancing Lipizzaners and Anglo-Arabians she had turned Issie's world upside down.

Francoise had recognised Blaze – only she said her name wasn't Blaze at all, it was Salome and she belonged to El Caballo Danza Magnifico. The mare had been stolen and now they wanted her back. Issie hadn't wanted to believe her, but Francoise had proof. The Frenchwoman was amazed that she had found the mare again. Issie had no choice but to agree to return her. She was totally devastated when Francoise took Blaze away. Then, just when Issie thought she'd lost her beloved mare forever, Blaze was unexpectedly returned to her once more. Francoise claimed that "a mysterious benefactor" had paid handsomely for the mare, with instructions that Blaze be given back to Issie.

Issie had never discovered who this "benefactor" was, or why they had bought her horse back. Whoever it was, she owed them a great debt and she knew it. Blaze was hers for always now. And despite all that had happened, Issie still considered Francoise to be her friend. After all, Francoise didn't own El Caballo Danza Magnifico – she just worked for them. Francoise loved horses as much as Issie did – she was the one who had trained Blaze and she truly understood just how special the bond was between Issie and her pony.

When Issie had found out that Blaze was pregnant and Marius was the father she had written immediately to Francoise D'arth to tell her the exciting news. Francoise hadn't replied, but Issie figured that was because she was away on tour with El Caballo Danza Magnifico. After Storm was born, Issie had written to Francoise again, sending photos this time – and still no reply. And now, suddenly out of the blue, here she was!

Francoise turned her gaze to the bay colt. "He is beautiful, Isadora. Everything you said about him in your letters was true." She ran her hand down Storm's legs, feeling the strength of his bone and muscle. She could not hide the fact that she was impressed by this colt. "He is even more beautiful than in your photos. This horse is destined for greatness."

"I'm glad you like him," said a rather stern voice. Issie turned round to see Tom Avery standing behind her. "Well, this is a surprise!" Avery said with a tone that indicated it was not an entirely pleasant one. "What are you doing here, Francoise?"

"Tom!" Francoise smiled warmly. "It is good to see you again. It has been too long." She stepped forward and greeted him with a kiss on both cheeks. Avery's face betrayed little emotion as he waited for Francoise to continue.

"When I got Isadora's letter telling me that Blaze was in foal to Marius I was so happy," Francoise said. "Then I received the next letter, saying that a foal had been born, and well, of course I was very intrigued. I had to come and meet this colt."

"Really?" Avery cocked an eyebrow at her. Issie noticed

that he still wasn't smiling. "Is that all, Francoise? It's a long way to come just to say hello. I have a feeling that there is something you aren't telling us."

Francoise's cheery smile faded and was replaced by a rather more serious expression.

"*Oui*. Yes. You are right, Tom. There is more to tell you – and much that we need to talk about."

"I thought there might be," Avery said. "El Caballo Danza Magnifico wouldn't send you all the way here just to check on this colt."

Francoise nodded. "You are right." She looked at the colt standing in front of her. "I was told to come here and see for myself whether this young horse was indeed the son of Marius." Francoise paused. "I was told that if Nightstorm had the same great conformation and temperament as his sire then I was to pay as much as you asked and bring him home to Spain."

"Francoise, I don't understand." Issie looked shocked. "You mean you want to buy Nightstorm?"

"*Oui*, Isadora," Francoise nodded. "El Caballo Danza Magnifico have told me that I must – and at any price!"

"But he's my horse! You can't—" Issie began, but Francoise interrupted her.

"Please, Isadora, be calm and listen," she implored.

"The people I work for are very wealthy. They are offering you a great deal of money. This colt, your Nightstorm, is the progeny of their best stallion Marius, and you know that your mare Blaze was once their most favoured of all. You can see how valuable a colt like this might be to the stable…"

"I don't care!" Issie said. She could feel the panic rising in her. She looked pleadingly at her instructor. "Tom? She has no right to take him away from me, does she?"

Avery's frown had deepened, but he said nothing. Issie felt as if her throat had closed over and she couldn't breathe. She was choking as she tried to force the words out.

"Tom!" Her voice was trembling now as she spoke. "Tell her! Storm is mine. They can't do this to me, not again!"

Issie had every reason to be nervous and she knew it. *After all*, she thought to herself, *the last time Francoise D'arth came to Chevalier Point I almost lost Blaze*. Now the Frenchwoman was back and Issie felt her world spiralling out of control once more. Would she lose Storm too?

Chapter 3

Tom Avery wasn't the sort of riding instructor who liked to raise his voice. He never shouted at his pupils; instead he spoke to them with measured, calm authority. It was this very same tone that he used now as he addressed Francoise D'arth.

"Isadora is right, Francoise," Avery said. "The colt is not for sale. I'm sorry you wasted your time on this trip, but I'm afraid you're going to have to go back to El Caballo and explain that Nightstorm can't be bought – at any price."

Francoise nodded solemnly. "If that is your decision I will accept it. But you do not understand everything yet – there is so much more I need to tell you both. We must talk further. May I come and see you again at the farm tomorrow?"

"There's no point in trying to change our minds," Avery said, "but you are our friend, Francoise, and you're welcome any time at Winterflood Farm."

Francoise smiled at this. "Thank you. I shall come over in the morning then, yes? At about nine?"

She glanced again at Nightstorm. The colt had begun to sense that something was going on. His nostrils were flared and he was pawing at the ground anxiously. As Issie reached for his halter to calm him, Nightstorm pulled back and let out a shrill whinny, his head held high and proud.

"Easy, Storm," Issie soothed, stroking his muzzle as the colt trembled with excitement beneath her hands.

"He is restless," Francoise said softly. "It is time for him to go home, yes?" She looked pointedly at Avery as she said this.

He nodded in agreement. "Yes, Francoise. You're right. Maybe it is."

That afternoon back at Winterflood Farm, Issie spent longer than usual grooming and feeding Storm. When she turned him out in his paddock she realised she didn't want to let the colt go. She gave him a long, snuggly hug, scratching him on the rump the way he liked, and stroking his velvet muzzle for ages before she finally slipped the halter off his head and set him loose.

"You're worried about him, aren't you?" Avery said when Issie finally came back to the stables.

"Yes," Issie said. "Aren't you?"

"I know it must be hard," Avery said gently, "after what happened the last time Francoise was here, and everything you went through with Blaze... But Issie, this isn't the same thing at all. Francoise has no claim over this colt. It doesn't matter what she says, Storm's your horse and nothing will change that." Avery reached over and ruffled her hair. "Now go home," he smiled. "I'll see you in the morning."

Mrs Brown took one look at Issie's face when she came through the front door and knew instantly that something was very wrong.

"I get the feeling it didn't go well at the pony club?" Mrs Brown asked.

Issie shook her head. "No, Mum, it went fine... but Francoise was there. She's in town. She's come to see Nightstorm."

Mrs Brown was surprised at this. "Francoise's in town? But I thought you hadn't even heard from her? What does she want?"

"She wants Nightstorm," Issie said. "She's offered to buy him. She's coming to the farm tomorrow morning to meet with me and Tom. We told her that Nightstorm wasn't for sale, but she said she had things to tell us…"

"What do you mean?"

"I don't know," Issie said, "but whatever it is, it can't be good."

Mrs Brown dropped the pile of laundry she had been sorting. "What on earth is Francoise playing at? First of all she doesn't even answer your letters and then she just turns up and demands that you sell her your horse? What time is she coming tomorrow? I can't wait to tell her myself that Storm isn't for sale and give her a piece of my mind!"

Issie shook her head. "It's OK, Mum. I can handle it. It isn't like that…" Issie couldn't believe she was defending Francoise, but in spite of everything she was still convinced that the Frenchwoman was her friend. "Tom has already told her Storm isn't for sale, we're just going to talk about stuff."

"Are you sure?" Mrs Brown arched a sceptical eyebrow.

"You don't need me to come too? You can always call me on my mobile if you like and I can—"

"Mum, really. I'll be OK," Issie managed a smile. "Tom will be there to back me up."

Mrs Brown didn't look convinced, but she let the matter drop and didn't bring it up again that evening.

Issie went to bed that night feeling utterly drained after everything that had happened. Once she was actually in bed, though, she couldn't sleep. She kept thinking about Francoise's strange comment. What did she mean when she said that she had so much more to tell them? Why was Nightstorm so important to El Caballo Danza Magnifico?

Despite her worries, she eventually dozed off, but she'd only been asleep a little while when her subconscious took over and the nightmare began. In her sleep, she tossed and turned, and vivid images flashed through her head as she relived that fateful day at the pony club. The day that Mystic died.

Mystic had been Issie's very first horse. With his swayed back and a dapple-grey coat that had faded with age, he was hardly the best-looking horse in the paddock at Chevalier Point. That didn't matter to Issie, though. She adored Mystic and thought he was the most beautiful horse ever. To her, Mystic would always be the horse that she had loved first, the one who had changed everything.

In her nightmare, Issie was back at the pony club, and it was the day of the accident. It was all happening again, in heart-wrenching slow motion. She saw Goldrush, Toby and Coco break loose, then panic and bolt for the pony-club gates. And then, before she could think it through, she was following on Mystic, galloping after them, trying to head them off before they reached the deadly main highway.

As they struck the road she heard the clean chime of Mystic's horseshoes on the tarmac. The ponies were ahead of them – at any moment they might be hit by a speeding car! She rode Mystic forward, circling the three horses and driving them back up the gravel driveway to the club grounds, getting them clear of the traffic and out of harm's way. Then suddenly Toby, Goldrush and Coco were gone and it was just Issie and Mystic all alone on the road. Issie could hear the low rumble of the truck, smell the diesel and hear the squeal of tyres as the massive vehicle tried to brake. Mystic turned to face the truck, like a stallion squaring up to his opponent, ready to fight. As he did so, he threw Issie back and out of the saddle. Issie felt herself falling. She knew what would happen next because she had been there before. She would be thrown clear of the truck, but Mystic, poor, brave Mystic, would face it head on. And he would die!

"Mystic, no! NO!" Issie screamed. She was still falling, but the ground seemed a long way away. Falling, falling and then — she woke up. Issie sat bolt upright in bed, her heart racing and her sheets soaked with sweat. She found herself gasping, trying to catch her breath, trying to fight back the tears, then giving up and crying again just like she had done that day when she'd woken up in the hospital bed and her mother told her that her pony was dead.

Issie's mum and everyone had tried to help her get over it, but how do you ever recover from losing your best friend? And so she'd sworn she would never ride again. The idea of loving another horse had just seemed impossible.

Then Tom Avery had turned up with Blaze. He told Issie about how the International League for the Protection of Horses had found the mare half-starved and maltreated. Issie knew then that she had no choice but to take the mare on. She poured her heart into helping Blaze and, as the mare got better, Issie's spirit recovered too.

Still, Issie never let go of her love for Mystic. And it turned out that the grey pony never let go of her either.

Issie had always known that her pony was special – but Mystic was much more special than anyone could have realised. He was like a guardian angel for Issie – and for Blaze. After the accident at the pony club, the grey gelding came back to Issie. He returned whenever she really needed him. Not as a ghost, but a real horse.

Mystic had a sixth sense for danger. He had saved Issie's life so many times now she had lost count.

She had dreamt about Mystic before. Her dreams were often a portent of what was to come. As she sat there in bed, Issie became aware of just what the dream meant. There was big danger afoot – she could feel it. A dream like that? It meant Mystic must be here.

Issie jumped out of her bed and raced to press her face up against the window. She peered out into the inky night, trying to see down to the garden below her room. It was raining outside, and large rivulets of water snaked down the pane of glass, blurring her view. There! Something was moving down on the lawn. It was hard to make the shape out clearly in the dark, but it was something big – Issie could see the shadow moving back and forth. Was it Mystic?

Pulling on a sweatshirt over her pyjamas, Issie raced down the stairs and out of the back door into the garden.

The rain was getting heavier now and the grass was squelchy and sodden under her feet.

"Mystic!" she hissed under her breath as she peered into the darkness. "Mystic!" It was so frustrating having to be quiet, but she didn't want to wake her mum.

Issie stood still for a moment, listening carefully. At first, all she could hear was her own heart beating. She began to doubt herself. Perhaps she had simply been having a nightmare. Maybe it didn't mean anything after all? She held her breath now and listened again.

There! She heard it. A soft nicker, the sound of a horse, coming from the far end of the garden. "Mystic!" Issie called again, her voice strained with emotion. This time she heard the whinny quite clearly, and then came the muffled sound of hoofbeats trotting towards her across the well-mown lawn. Out of the darkness, a dapple-grey horse stepped forward to meet her.

"Mystic!"

The bad dream had left Issie so shaken-up that the sight of her pony actually standing right there in front of her made her instantly burst into tears once more. She wiped her cheeks roughly with her sweatshirt sleeve. She had to pull herself together.

"Hey boy," she murmured. She put out her hand to

touch her beloved pony and for a brief moment she wondered if Mystic would disappear again, nothing more than a misty shadow in the rain. Then she felt her fingers close around the coarse, ropey strands of Mystic's long, silver mane, and her hands touched the soft warmth of his dappled coat.

"Hey, Mystic, did you miss me?" Issie smiled. She was so desperately pleased to see her pony, yet his presence sent a chill through her heart. Issie realised immediately that if Mystic was here, then something was wrong. Very wrong.

The grey gelding seemed tense and anxious. He turned away from the house and began to trot back down the lawn towards the far end of the garden. Issie had seen him do this before and she knew exactly what he wanted her to do. Pulling on her boots, she followed him in the darkness, heading for the gate at the end that led to the street. Issie swung the gate open, taking hold of the pony by his mane so that he stood parallel to it. Then she climbed the wooden gate to the third rung and, without a second thought about what she was doing, leapt on to the grey pony's back.

Issie took a moment to get her balance, then tapped the pony lightly with her heels. He responded instantly, moving off at a brisk trot. As soon as they reached the grass verge of the road, Issie urged Mystic on from a trot into a loping canter. She had no saddle and the canter was less bouncy and easier to ride bareback. Issie had no reins either, but it didn't matter. She could have guided Mystic with her legs, but she knew better than to try and steer the pony. After all, Mystic had come to her with a warning and that meant he knew exactly where he was going. All Issie needed to do was wrap her hands into his long mane and hang on.

She gripped his mane tightly and bent down low over his neck as the rain began to fall harder. She realised she had been stupid to race out in weather like this, without changing into her jodhpurs and raincoat. Already she was chilled to the bone as the wind whipped her icy skin and the rain soaked her pyjamas. It was too late to worry about that now, though. Beneath her, Mystic's canter was almost hypnotic, rhythmic and steady, as his hooves pounded a tempo on the grass verge. There was no turning back.

Issie still had no idea where they were going. It wasn't until they had been riding for almost ten minutes when she saw tall rows of poplar trees rising up in front of them and realised they had reached the banks of the river. As Mystic turned along the esplanade she guessed they were heading towards Winterflood Farm. She felt a chill up her spine. *Nightstorm was at Winterflood Farm.* This couldn't be a coincidence – the arrival of Francoise D'arth and now Mystic? No. It was clear that all of this had something to do with the bay colt.

Beneath her, Mystic's strides lengthened as he reached the wide grass strip that ran along the banks of the river. They had ridden this path once before in the dark and Issie had trusted Mystic then to get her there, just as she did now. Instead of trying to slow the grey pony down, she leant down low over Mystic's neck and let him gallop. If Nightstorm really was in danger then they had to move fast. There wasn't a moment to lose.

Minutes later, the clatter of Mystic's hooves on the gravel driveway announced their arrival at Winterflood Farm. As Mystic slowed to a trot, Issie vaulted off his back and hit the ground running. She sprinted around the side of Avery's house, taking the short cut past the tack room and out the back of the house. She had put Nightstorm in the magnolia paddock when they came back from pony club. Her eyes flitted across the paddock now. She couldn't see the colt anywhere.

"Storm?" Issie's voice was trembling as she called out to the colt. "Storm?"

She fought her rising panic, took a deep breath, pursed

her lips and blew. Once, and then a second time. Storm always came when she whistled.

Issie strained her eyes in the darkness, looking for the colt. She couldn't see a thing. She tried shouting out his name again.

This time, the lights in the house went on and a few moments later Tom Avery emerged from the back door.

"Issie? I thought I heard you…" Avery was half asleep on the back porch of the cottage, tying his dressing gown and rubbing his eyes. "What on earth are you doing? It's the middle of the night!"

"Tom?" Issie said. "Where's Nightstorm? He's not in his paddock."

Avery shook his head.

"The weather report was for thunderstorms so I moved him inside. He's in the stables…"

Before Avery had finished speaking Issie was already moving, running hard towards the stables. Avery shouted something else after her, but she couldn't make out what he said. All she could hear was the rush of her own heartbeat, pounding in her ears.

When she reached the stables, she realised that Avery must have gone back inside to switch on the mains for the stable lights because they suddenly flickered to life above her head. There were three loose boxes in Avery's stables. The two at the far end were open and empty, but the one closest to the entrance was bolted shut. This was the stall that Avery usually kept Storm in, and Issie raced towards it now. With trembling fingers, she tried to open the door and was driven into a frenzy of frustration when she found that her hands were so numb from the cold it was impossible to work the bolt loose.

"Here!" A voice said. "It gets stuck sometimes. Better let me do it." Avery was standing behind her. He was dressed in his boots and an oilskin, which he must have stopped to pull on before following her, and Issie suddenly realised how mad she must look in comparison, standing here in her soaking-wet pyjamas and sweatshirt in the middle of the night. She stood aside and let Avery step forward to work the bolt loose and swing the stall door open.

When Avery opened the door Issie felt stunned disbelief. She had been expecting to find her colt injured or sick, but instead she was staring at an empty stall.

"I don't understand!" Avery said. "I locked him in myself!"

Maybe I'm still asleep, Issie thought, *maybe this isn't real. It's all part of the dream*. She wished it were true, but the prickle of the goosebumps on her freezing skin told her otherwise. She was wide awake and she understood now why Mystic had come to her tonight. She had dreamt that she was losing her horse, the most precious thing in the world. Now, in a sickening rush, she realised the nightmare was real. Once again, she had lost the thing that was most precious to her. She was too late. Nightstorm was gone.

Chapter 4

A quick investigation of the stables by Avery confirmed their suspicions that the colt had been stolen.

"Whoever it was must have broken into the tack shed as well," he said as he rejoined Issie. "They've used boltcutters to get in, but they didn't take anything – except Nightstorm's halter."

Avery looked at Issie, who was shaking like a leaf in her dripping-wet pyjamas. "You must be freezing!" he said. "We'd better get inside. We're not helping Nightstorm standing out here. We have to figure out what to do next."

Issie didn't move. When she finally spoke her words came out in a stutter because she was shivering, her lips blue and trembling from the cold. "We… we… need to find Francoise."

Issie and Avery were both thinking the same thing. Nightstorm's disappearance had to be connected to the sudden arrival of Francoise D'arth. The question was, how exactly was the mysterious Frenchwoman involved?

While Issie dried herself off and changed into one of Avery's sweatshirts and a pair of tracksuit bottoms, Avery phoned the number that Francoise had given them the day before when they'd met at the pony club.

Issie could hear him speaking briefly on the phone. She finished getting dressed, rolling up the sleeves of the sweatshirt so that her hands were poking out of the ends, and came into the kitchen to find Avery putting the kettle on.

"I'm making us some coffee to warm you up," he said. "You were like a block of ice out there in your pyjamas. How did you end up here in the middle of the night, anyway?"

"I... ummm... I had a bad dream," Issie said. "I guess I was half asleep when I left home, and I didn't think of getting changed and... anyway, what did Francoise say? Did you speak to her?"

"You could say that."

"What do you mean?"

"It was a pretty quick conversation. I told her what had happened and she said to wait for her to arrive before we did anything," Avery said. "She's on her way here now."

"Shouldn't we call the police too?" Issie said.

Avery shook his head. "She made me promise to wait until she arrived."

They didn't have long to wait. Francoise must have driven to Winterflood Farm like a demon, because by the time Avery was pouring the coffee they could hear her car pulling up in the driveway outside. Francoise swept into the living room. There were none of the usual cheek kisses or *bonjours* – she was tense as a cat that was about to pounce. Her face was dark with fury.

"When did this happen?" she demanded. "How long has the colt been missing?"

"Hey!" Avery said. "I think we're the ones who should be asking the questions here, Francoise. From the way you're acting now it's obvious you knew that the colt was in danger. Who's taken him? Is it someone from El Caballo Danza Magnifico? Is that why you're here?"

Francoise seemed deeply offended by this accusation. "Of course not! How could you even think that El Caballo would do something like that?"

"Well," Avery said, "it's a bit of a coincidence, don't you think? You turn up here one day offering to buy the colt and now he's gone? I think you need to tell us, Francoise. What's going on?"

Francoise shook her head. "We don't have time for explanations," she insisted. "For every moment that we speak they are getting further away with the colt."

"All right," Avery said. "If we don't have much time, then you'd better explain fast, Francoise. Tell me everything and then I'm calling the police."

"No! No police!" Francoise instructed. "I know these men and they are ruthless. If they think the police are involved they will kill Nightstorm. I will call my contacts and see what can be done, but I suspect it is probably too late. By now they will already have him on the plane."

"Plane?" Issie felt as if all the air had suddenly been sucked out of the room. She couldn't breathe, she couldn't think. What was going on here? What was Francoise talking about? "Francoise? What's happened to Nightstorm? Where is my horse?"

The Frenchwoman looked at Issie. "Isadora. I can understand how this looks, but believe me, El Caballo Danza Magnifico did not take your Nightstorm. But you are right, I do have something to do with this. When

I told you yesterday that I had been sent by El Caballo Danza Magnifico I was telling the truth. They sent me here to buy Nightstorm and bring him back to Spain. However, I did not tell you that I was also sent here to protect the colt."

"Protect him? Protect him from who?" Issie was confused.

"When I told my riders at El Caballo Danza Magnifico that Blaze was having Marius's foal, they were so excited," Francoise said. "In fact, soon the news of Nightstorm's birth was the talk of the local village." She shook her head ruefully. "Harmless gossip – or so I thought at the time. I didn't see the danger in it. I was stupid. I should have known that once certain men found out, they would do anything to get their hands on a colt born with such a bloodline."

"Do you mean one of the staff at El Caballo has taken him?" Issie asked.

"No, no!" Francoise seemed frustrated that no one grasped what she was saying. "Not from our farm. It is our rivals who have taken the colt! El Caballo Danza Magnifico is not the only great stud farm in Andalusia. There are others that also breed horses. These horsemen know only too well how valuable the progeny of a stallion as great as Marius can be. Especially now, with the race so near, and so much to lose…"

"Race? What are you talking about?" Avery shook his head in bewilderment. "Listen, Francoise, I know you say time is running out, but if these men already have Nightstorm on a plane to Europe then there's no way we can catch them now. Let's all take a deep breath. I think you'd better tell us everything, and start at the beginning this time."

Francoise looked as if she was about to argue with Avery, but then let out a heavy sigh, as if admitting defeat. "You are right. It is too late anyway to stop them. We might as well speak about this now." She shook her head sorrowfully. "I intended to tell you everything when I came here this morning, but not under these circumstances. This development is most unfortunate."

"You could put it that way," Avery said darkly. Then he softened. "I was making coffee just now. Would you like some?"

"*Oui*, yes please." Francoise managed a weak smile as she pulled out a chair and sat down at the kitchen table. Issie sat beside her while Avery poured them all a cup of coffee, and Francoise began her story.

"In Andalusia, where El Caballo Danza Magnifico has its stables, there are many famous horse estates, or *haciendas* as we know them in Spain. Each hacienda, of course, believes that they breed the best horses in the world." Francoise took a sip of her coffee and continued. "Over the centuries there have been many arguments over whose stable had the very best horses of all. And then one day, many decades ago, the haciendas joined together and decided to find out once and for all."

"And so they held a race?" Issie said.

"*Oui*, exactly," Francoise continued, "but not just any race, Isadora. This race was held in the middle of the village square, near the Sierra de Grazalema mountains. Twelve stables were invited to enter a horse in the race. One horse and one rider from each of the twelve, representing the most prominent and prestigious stud farms in Andalusia. The winning stable would be proven to have the best horses in all of Spain." Francoise paused. "There was much at stake in this race. To win meant great honour. To lose, to fail in this race meant great misfortune for your stable. You see, the winner would be allowed to handpick five of the very best horses from each of the other eleven haciendas. Imagine that! If you lost the race you would lose your greatest treasure – the best five horses in your herd!"

Francoise saw the look on Issie's face as she realised what this meant.

"You see how important this race is," she continued. "The winning hacienda would strengthen their bloodlines with the best horses from each of their rivals' stables."

Avery interrupted, "I've heard of this race, Francoise. They call it the race for the Silver Bridle. But I thought it was just a legend, something the *vaqueros*, the Spanish cowboys, took part in a long time ago."

Francoise shook her head. "The race is not dead. It has continued throughout the generations – it happens every ten years. Even now, in modern times, the race is as important as it ever was. Each stable wants desperately to win."

"And now the race is here again?" Issie asked.

"*Oui*," Francoise said. "Yes, Isadora. It is here again. El Caballo Danza Magnifico have selected the best horse in our stables, the stallion Marius, to run for us. If he wins, then we may take our pick of all the best bloodlines from the best stables in Andalusia. If he loses, then we lose our best horses too, just like the rest."

"I still don't understand," Issie said. "What does this have to do with Nightstorm? He's only a colt. He's far too young to race."

"You are right, of course," Francoise said. "He is too young to run. But he is the son of Marius – his bloodlines are beyond value. If we do lose the race then the winning stable will choose our best five horses to take. I do not doubt that they will choose Marius. We have only one other foal by him and he will get chosen also. And then where will that leave us? That is why I was sent here. At least if we had your colt then we would have a son of Marius and the bloodline could continue." Francoise looked worried. "Unfortunately, I was not the only one who realised this. Another rival hacienda had the same idea. Only they did not come here to buy your colt. They came to steal him."

"What will they do with him?" Issie asked.

"They will take him back to Spain, where they will hide him at their stud farm until the race is over," Francoise said. "You are right, Tom – I hate to admit it, but there is no point in trying to stop them now. These men will have been watching, planning and anticipating us, and will already have him on a plane. They have much money and great resources. They know the value of the son of Marius and they will stop at nothing to get him."

"But they can't just steal my horse and get away with it!" Issie couldn't believe what she was hearing. "Even if they get Nightstorm back to Spain, the police there must be able to arrest them!"

Avery agreed. "We should call Interpol. The international police. They must be able to act, force these men to give Nightstorm back."

Francoise shook her head. "And how will you prove to them that he is your colt? He has no brand, no microchipping, no papers. It seems unlikely, does it not, that a young girl in New Zealand would own one of the best Spanish colts with the finest bloodlines in Andalusia? No. Without proof that the colt is yours, the police will never believe you."

"Then what do you suggest?" Avery asked.

"I suggest that you leave it to me," Francoise said. "El Caballo Danza Magnifico will get Nightstorm back. We too have great resources – and we also have much to lose."

Much to lose? Issie couldn't believe it. Surely no one had more to lose than she did? Storm was her colt. She thought about how he must be feeling right now, all alone in a horse box, being loaded on to a plane, wondering where Issie was, feeling scared.

Issie was scared too, but at that moment she realised she had to put her fears aside. She had to be brave. Storm needed her.

"I want to come!" The words came as a shock to her even as she blurted them out.

"What?" Francoise was confused.

"Take me with you to Spain. If this rival stable, whoever they are, has my colt, then I'm coming with you to get him back."

"Impossible," Francoise stated firmly. "It is too dangerous. It is best that you leave this to us."

"Storm is the one who's in danger! He's never even been away from home without me before. He must be terrified!" Issie was shaking, not with the cold this time, but with anger. "I can't stay here and do nothing while they have him. I have to try and get him back. Please, Francoise."

Francoise turned to Avery for support. "Tell her that she is being ridiculous, Tom."

"I wish I could, Francoise," Avery replied, "but I'm afraid I'm on Issie's side. We can't be expected to wait here, not knowing what has happened to Nightstorm. If we come with you, surely there is a chance that we can negotiate directly with these men. We can make them see sense. I certainly think it's better than sitting here and doing nothing."

"We?" Francoise looked at him. "So now you are coming too?"

"It looks that way, doesn't it?"

Francoise sighed and shook her head. "You are both

impossible, I think. But you are also right. I would do the same if I were you. I will book the air tickets. El Caballo Danza Magnifico will pay your fares. There is a plane leaving tomorrow night. We should be on it. Pack your bags, and organise your passports. I will call you with details later and meet you at the airport."

And with that, Francoise disappeared out the door. There was the sound of her car squealing on the gravel driveway outside and she was gone.

"Well," Avery said, looking at Issie. "Looks like we're off to Spain then." His face dropped suddenly and Issie could tell from his expression that he had just remembered something. "Don't you have school tomorrow?"

Issie did have school tomorrow. In fact she had another whole week of school to go before the winter-term break. However, this was the least of her problems. She might have been able to convince Francoise to let her come to Spain, but convincing her mum to let her go halfway around the world to track down the horse thieves who had taken her colt? That would be flat-out impossible.

"Let me speak to your mother," Avery suggested. "I'm sure if I explain she'll listen to me."

"You must be kidding!"

It turned out that Avery was being a little optimistic when he said that Mrs Brown would listen to him. They had woken her at 6 a.m. and tried to put her in a good mood before they popped the question by making her breakfast. But it soon became clear that it would take more than bacon and eggs to bring her round.

"You expect me to let Isadora go to Spain with you to hunt down horse thieves?" Mrs Brown shook her head in disbelief. "Tom! This is crazy and you know it!"

"Mrs B," Avery began, "it's perfectly safe. We'll go over there and prove the colt is ours, talk to the authorities if necessary..." He locked eyes with Issie's mum. "Amanda, you must trust me. You know I would never put Isadora in any danger. But this is the best chance we have of getting the colt back."

"Why don't you just call the authorities and let them handle it?" Mrs Brown said.

"Call who exactly? Interpol aren't going to chase around Andalusia to get a girl's horse back for her!" Avery said. "Believe me, Amanda, if I thought there was any other way..."

Mrs Brown shook her head. "Then maybe we have no choice, Tom. Maybe we'll just have to let Nightstorm go."

Issie felt the blood freeze in her veins. "Mum? You can't mean that!"

"Issie, I can't let you go over there by yourself!"

"But I won't be going by myself!" Issie said. "Tom will be there, and Francoise too! They'll look after me. And I'll call you every day."

"This is madness, Issie. Apart from anything else you'll be missing school."

"Last week of term is just a muck-about week, Mum — everyone knows that. I've finished all my work." Issie looked at her mother with pleading eyes. "I'm fourteen years old. I'm old enough to do this."

"You're still my baby," Mrs Brown objected.

"And Storm is my baby," Issie countered, "and he's out there right now on his own and he's probably terrified. He needs me." She paused. "Mum, I can't leave him with those men. I can't just pretend that Nightstorm doesn't exist and go on with life. He belongs here, with me and with Blaze. I have to get him back. And you have to let me go."

Mrs Brown looked at her daughter's face, the strong determined set of her jaw, and the fierce wilfulness that burned in her. They were so alike, mother and daughter — both with their long, dark hair, willowy limbs and olive skin. But there were differences between them too – Issie was so headstrong, and so independent, just like her Aunty Hester. Mrs Brown was always amazed by the ferocity of the passion that her daughter possessed. Her love for her horses was beyond anything she had ever seen before. At that moment Mrs Brown realised that if she prevented Issie from doing this, she would be destroying that passion, crushing the spirit out of her daughter. No matter how painful, how terrifying it was, she had to make a choice.

"Issie," she said softly. "I hope I'm not going to regret this…"

"Mum! Please—" Issie began to argue, but her mother raised a hand.

"Don't," she said, shaking her head. "Don't fight me, Isadora. Just listen… because I'm telling you that I'm going to let you go."

Chapter 5

The man behind the glass wall gave Issie a stern look as she approached him, dragging her suitcase. "Documents!" he snapped as she fumbled in her pockets and pulled out her airline ticket and her papers. His expression softened when he opened her passport.

"You are from New Zealand?" He raised an eyebrow. "It is a long way to come to Madrid – halfway around the world!" His strict face broke into a kindly smile.

It had been a long way. Twenty-four hours in the plane without a proper stop. Over that time Issie had watched five movies and eaten three dinners – the plane never seemed to serve lunch or breakfast, it was nothing but never-ending dinnertime.

Issie's inner body clock felt completely mixed up by the

time they landed in Madrid. It was midday in Spain, which meant that right now, back home in New Zealand, it was midnight. Even weirder, she suddenly found herself baking hot. It was summer! Issie couldn't believe it. Yesterday she had been freezing in the cold and rain of winter, and now here she was on the other side of the world and it was a glorious, sunny day.

Francoise had warned Issie to pack for the summer heat with T-shirts and shorts, but she had still boarded the plane in her winter clothes. As she emerged from the air-conditioned airport on to the street outside she began to swelter instantly in her sweatshirt and jeans. The long flight had left her feeling sticky and exhausted. Her brain was swimming, and she was finding it hard to think straight.

"You've got jetlag," Avery told her. "Did you sleep at all on the plane?"

Issie had tried to sleep, but every time she closed her eyes all she could think about was Storm. Where was the colt now? Was he already here in Spain? Did horses get jetlag too? Did Storm feel just like she did? She wished she could be there with him, to let him know it was going to be OK, that she was coming for him and that she was going to bring him home again.

"We'd better get moving," Francoise said as they wheeled their suitcases through customs. "The next train from Madrid to Seville leaves in less than an hour."

The train station in Madrid turned out to be a giant tropical glasshouse. In the centre of it, enormous palm trees sprouted out of the ground, their thick, green leaves creating a jungle canopy. It wasn't like any train station Issie had ever seen. And the train wasn't like anything she had ever seen either. It was shaped like a space rocket.

"It goes like a rocket too!" Francoise laughed when Issie told her this. "Three hundred kilometres an hour. We'll be in Seville in a couple of hours from now and from there we drive on to El Caballo Danza Magnifico."

Tiredness finally overwhelmed Issie as they settled into their seats and she curled up, using her bag as a pillow, to be rocked asleep by the steady rhythm of the train.

It felt like she had only just drifted off when she was being woken up again, Avery's hand on her shoulder shaking her gently. "Issie, we're here."

Groggy from her nap, Issie followed Francoise out to the street.

"Alfie is supposed to be meeting us with the car," Francoise said as she scanned the parking lot. Her face broke into a broad smile as she spied a beaten-up old

Land Rover heading towards them. "There he is!"

The Land Rover pulled up and the boy behind the wheel gave a cheery wave before opening the door and leaping out to join them on the pavement. "Alfie!" Francoise gave the boy a kiss on both cheeks. "These are my friends, Isadora and Tom."

She turned to introduce the boy to them. "This is Alfonso. He is head of the stables at El Caballo Danza Magnifico." Issie's first thought when she'd seen Alfonso pull up in the Land Rover was that he looked a little bit like Aidan. He was about Aidan's age, with the same mop of dark hair. Now that he was standing right in front of her, Issie realised that Alfonso didn't really look like Aidan at all. He was much more tanned, and he had dark brown eyes that smiled readily whenever he did. His features were different from Aidan's too. Aidan's face was delicate and fine-boned, while this boy had the broad, rugged looks of a Spanish film star.

If he was good-looking though, Issie didn't really notice. It was sad but true that she was pretty much too lovesick over Aidan to look at any other boy. This wouldn't have been so sad if it weren't for the fact that she hadn't even seen him since he'd kissed her goodbye that day on the cherry tree lawn at Blackthorn Farm. It was so unfair, Issie thought, to finally, officially have a boyfriend, and never get to actually be near him. She longed to gaze once more into those pale blue eyes that Aidan kept half hidden under that long, dark fringe…

"Issie?" She was shaken out of her Aidan daydream by the sound of Avery's voice intruding sharply into her thoughts.

"Issie!" The voice prodded a second time. "Wake up! I said to give your bag to Alfonso so he can load it into the car."

"Sorry." Issie shook herself back to reality and reached out to hand Alfonso her bag. "I guess I'm a bit jetlagged."

Alfonso gave Issie a broad grin and took her bag.

"That's OK," he said. "How was your trip? Was the food on the plane actually, like, food, or was it totally gross?"

"You speak English!" Issie exclaimed with relief. She didn't know any Spanish and had been terribly worried that she wouldn't be able to understand a word that anyone said.

"Yeah," Alfonso said casually, "I picked it up from touring with El Caballo – we're overseas a lot with the horses so most of us know lots of languages. We can all speak English really well." He picked up Issie's bag and threw it in the back of the Land Rover and opened the passenger door for her. "Come on, *vamos*!" he said.

Issie looked at him blankly and didn't move.

"*Vamos* – that means 'let's go'!" Francoise laughed as she offered Issie the front seat next to Alfonso. Francoise and Avery climbed into the back seat, Alfonso put his foot down on the accelerator and the Land Rover roared into life, heading down the cobbled streets, making its way through the busy city towards the outskirts of town.

Within an hour they had left Seville and the Land Rover began to climb through the forest-clad hills of Andalusia. As Alfonso turned off the main road, pale dust flew up from beneath the car tyres and they began to make their way along remote dirt tracks through the rugged farmland that led to El Caballo Danza Magnifico. The Land Rover bumped and skipped along the potholed road, dust flying in through the open windows. Issie clung on to her seatbelt to stop herself being thrown about as the car bounced around.

Issie looked over at Alfonso, who was focused on the road. "You know, you don't look old enough to be driving this car, and you certainly don't look old enough to be the head of the stables."

Alfonso raised an eyebrow. "You're not happy with my driving?"

"No, I didn't mean that!" Issie stammered. "I'm sorry, that came out sounding really rude! I just meant—"

Alfonso grinned. "It's OK. I'm just joking. You're right. I'm only eighteen. Most of the riders at El Caballo are much older than me. But I've been in the saddle since the day I was born. It is in my blood."

Francoise leaned forward from the back seat to explain. "Alfie is the son of Roberto Nunez, the owner of El Caballo Danza Magnifico. Roberto is one of Spain's greatest horsemen. He once rode for the Spanish eventing team at the Olympics. As a rider in this country his career remains unrivalled."

"But your dad doesn't ride any more?" Issie said.

"Yeah, he still rides," Alfonso shrugged. "He's the one responsible for training all of our best stallions for the performing school. But he doesn't like to tour. He prefers the quiet life here in Spain with the herd."

"Will Roberto be there when we arrive?" Avery asked.

Alfonso nodded. "He went out this morning to bring in some of the mares, but he should be there to meet us when we get to the hacienda. It's not much further now. We'll be there soon. We're already on land that belongs to El Caballo. These olive trees that you see around you were planted by us. We grow oranges and olives here in the dry hills and the horses graze down in the valley, where the pasture is better."

"How long have you lived here?" Issie asked.

"All my life," Alfonso replied. "El Caballo has been my family's home for two centuries."

Francoise spoke up again from the back seat. "This place is steeped in tradition. When I left France and the Cadre Noir de Saumur to come and work here, I did not realise how long it would take to be accepted." Francoise laughed. "For the first five years they would call me 'the new girl'. It was a joke, of course, but it took them a long time to grow tired of it. Then, finally, one day, they said 'she is one of us now'. I have been here for ten years, and sometimes I still feel like I am the new girl…"

As Francoise was talking the Land Rover had been bumping and bouncing its way along the dirt road through the olive-clad hills. Now, as they came over the crest of the range, Issie looked down into the valley below. The sight that greeted her was one of the most beautiful she had seen in her entire life. The sunburnt fields were dotted with snow-white horses, mares with their coal-black foals at foot. To see these horses running free as a herd was like bringing a fairy story to life.

"Ohmygod! They are so beautiful!" Issie breathed.

Francoise nodded. "They are the very best mares. Roberto has a true eye for horses and it is his mastery that has made El Caballo Danza Magnifico stables the most respected in all of Spain. We have almost fifty horses here – stallions, mares and foals. Roberto loves his Spanish-bred Lipizzaners and also the Andalusians and his prized Anglo-Arabs – the bloodline of your mare Blaze."

The beauty of the horses was almost eclipsed by the sight of El Caballo itself. The grand, classical Spanish buildings of the hacienda were arranged around a cobbled courtyard with palm trees and fountains, and surrounding the estate was a high wall made of whitewashed stone. The entrance was marked by enormous black wrought-iron gates, which Alfonso drove through while Francoise pointed out the four main buildings of the hacienda.

"I will give you the full tour later," she said, "but in the meantime, let me quickly explain." She pointed to the building straight ahead of them. It was a rich golden mustard colour, the same colour, Issie noted, as the dirt under their car tyres. "That is the mares' stable block," Francoise said. Issie peered at the Spanish arches and could make out rows of loose boxes inside, set into archways of mosaic tiles.

Francoise gestured to the building next to it, which was larger still, with whitewashed walls this time, edged in the same mustard-ochre hue. "Our indoor arena is bigger than an Olympic arena," Francoise said. "We need as much space as possible to train the horses in the *haute école* movements and routines for our shows."

On the other side of this arena was yet another stable block with Spanish archways at the front. "The stallions' stables," Francoise explained. "We like to keep their quarters at a distance from the mares, of course."

Alfonso drove around the fountain, doing a lap of the courtyard, and then pulled the car up outside the front door of the most beautiful of all the buildings. It was a two-storey, stately Spanish villa, also with a grand archway surrounding the front door. To one side of the entrance, vines of brilliant orange and hot-pink bougainvillea grew against the white walls, their blooms splashing the villa with brilliant colour. Wrought-iron window boxes on the top floor were filled with candy-pink geraniums, spilling out and tumbling over the ledges. Seville orange trees groomed and shaped into tall topiary, stood on either side of the front steps that led to the door.

"This is the main house. You will be staying here with us for the duration of your visit," Francoise said.

Issie stepped out of the car and gazed around her in

disbelief. She smiled at Avery. "Can you believe this place?" she asked.

"I've heard a lot about it, but I've never—" Avery began, but he was interrupted by the rumble of horses galloping towards them.

Francoise looked up at the wrought-iron gates of the compound. "That will be Roberto now. He is bringing in the Anglo-Arabian mares from the far fields in the upper pasture where they have been grazing for the past weeks."

The rumble grew louder, and then suddenly Issie saw the first of the Anglo-Arabs appear through El Caballo's entranceway. For a moment her heart leapt – the mare cantering towards her across the cobbled courtyard looked just like Blaze! She was a deep liver chestnut, with a flaxen blonde mane and tail. Behind the mare ran half a dozen others just like her, some of them with matching colts and fillies at their feet. Issie's smile grew wide as she gazed at the beauty of these mares. They seemed to know exactly where they were going, trotting obediently through the main gates and across the courtyard to the stable block, each of them choosing a different archway to duck and weave through as they headed towards their loose boxes.

"They are like homing pigeons!" Francoise grinned.

Issie heard the crack of a stock whip at the gates and

saw that there were three men on horseback following the golden chestnut mares. Two of these men were on bay Andalusian horses, beautiful animals with long flowing black manes and elegant arched necks. The third man rode the most beautiful horse, an enormous dapple-grey stallion with a high-stepping trot and the most graceful physique of them all. Issie knew the stallion on sight – it was Marius! Nightstorm's sire.

The man riding Marius gave orders in Spanish to the other two riders, who followed in on their horses after the mares. Then he wheeled the great, grey stallion about on his hocks and cantered gracefully over to the steps of the villa where Francoise, Alfonso, Issie and Avery stood.

He leapt down out of the saddle and smiled at Issie. He was a handsome man, with the dark, swarthy skin of a Spaniard, kind eyes and thick waves of black hair. Tall and lean, he wore cream jodhpurs and long black boots. On the pocket of his white shirt a red C had been embroidered with the shape of a red heart set inside it. It was the same symbol, Issie realised, that she had seen branded on the haunches of the horses as they raced in to their stalls. The same symbol too, was printed in blood-red on the golden flag that flew at the gates of the compound. Of course! The C with the heart in the middle was the brand of El Caballo Danza Magnifico, Issie realised. And this man standing in front of them now had to be the owner of El Caballo Danza Magnifico, Roberto Nunez.

Roberto's smile faded and he looked serious as he locked eyes with Tom Avery. The Spaniard walked past Issie, Alfonso and Francoise and strode directly towards Avery, his face an unreadable mask. He came closer and closer until the two men were almost nose to nose, and then suddenly his face broke into a broad grin.

"Thomas! It has been so long! Too long!" His broad hands grabbed Avery by the shoulders and gave him a shake before he enclosed Avery in a swift bear hug.

The others stood there in stunned amazement as Avery, normally so cool and aloof, hugged him back. "Hello Roberto," Avery said warmly. "It's good to see you again."

"You two know each other?" Issie couldn't believe it.

"Know each other?" Roberto laughed. "Did this old devil not tell you?" He grinned and put an arm around Avery. "This man," he said, "this man, he is my brother!"

Chapter 6

Issie was stunned. Avery was Roberto's brother?

Roberto grinned. "Thomas and I haven't seen each other for twenty years. We met at the World Equestrian Games at Stockholm, Sweden. I was a brash young man, riding for the honour of Spain. Thomas was riding there too – he was the favourite to win against me in the three-day eventing." Roberto turned to Avery. "It was on the cross-country course there that this man gave up the chance for a medal in order to save my life. This is why I say that he is a brother to me. I trust him completely and I shall never forget the debt that I owe him."

Avery shook his head. "You don't owe me anything, Roberto. Anyway, that debt has been repaid many times since with your kindness."

"Wait a minute!" Alfonso was amazed. "You're *the* Tom Avery? Wow! Dad has talked about you for years. I never realised when he sent me to pick up someone called Tom from the train that it would be you. Dad has told me the most amazing stories about you."

"Stories? What kind of stories?" Issie was in shock. To her, Tom Avery was just her pony-club instructor. Sure, he was great with horses and everything, but the idea of him being some kind of legendary figure in this Spanish household was going to take some getting used to. "Why have you never told me before now that you were friends with the man who owned El Caballo Danza Magnifico?"

Avery gave her a wry grin. "I still have a few secrets left, Isadora."

"Issie is not the only one here who is surprised," Francoise said tartly. "Roberto did not mention this to me either."

"Oh, I did not want to bore you with stories of my glory days, Francoise," Roberto smiled. He looked at Issie. "But this is very rude of me! We should not be standing here on the doorstep. Where are my manners? Young lady, you must be tired after your long journey. Come inside! Francoise will show you to your room so that you can freshen up after your long trip." Roberto Nunez gestured towards the front door of the villa. "The guest rooms are ready and waiting. I will give you a chance to settle in. I have work to do myself this afternoon – we can all meet again to talk later at dinner."

Issie stepped inside the front door of the villa and found it to be even grander than she expected. The polished wood floors were strewn with elaborate Moorish rugs, the walls were painted in bright, earthy shades of ochre and tangerine and covered with antique tapestries and paintings of horses.

"Follow me," Francoise instructed, leading Issie past the living room, filled with vases of fresh roses, then the grand dining room and finally the library, its walls lined with books, before they reached the staircase which led to the guest rooms upstairs.

"I hope you will be comfortable here," Francoise said, opening the door. The room was beautiful. The walls were rustic plaster, washed in deepest pink, and the bed was covered with rainbow-striped blankets. Enormous mirrors trimmed with silver frames sparkled and glittered in the sunlight that streamed through the wide glass doors leading out to a private balcony.

"Do you like it?" Francoise crossed the room and drew back the rainbow-striped curtains to reveal a view of the cobbled courtyard below.

"It's amazing!" Issie said. "Everything is amazing. It's so beautiful here!"

"It is, isn't it?" Francoise said, gazing out over the hacienda. "When we travel away on tour with the horses we are gone for such a long time, and then to come home to this – it always makes my heart leap when we return here."

She pointed towards the stable blocks. "You see over there where we keep the mares? Salome – I mean Blaze – was born right there in those stables, in one of the foaling stalls."

Issie stared out of the window and felt a shiver up her spine. She knew Blaze was an El Caballo mare, but it had never occurred to her before now that this farm had once been Blaze's home. Her beautiful chestnut mare was actually born and schooled here, just as the rest of El Caballo's horses were.

"I remember I had only just started working for El Caballo back then," Francoise said dreamily. "It was foaling season and the mares due to have their babies were brought in each night, and I would sleep in the stables, to keep a close eye on them. Blaze's dam, Bahiyaa, was the most beautiful of all the mares in our stables so we were all waiting with great excitement to see what her foal would be like. We were not disappointed

– when Blaze was born we knew immediately that she was special. Oh, she was the most beautiful foal! I wish you could have seen her then! To witness the arrival of a new life, to see a new foal being born, it is so magical."

Issie's smile melted away as Francoise spoke. She too knew what it was like to be the one to deliver a newborn foal. When Blaze had foaled, it was Issie alone who had been there to help Nightstorm enter the world. In the excitement of her arrival here at El Caballo Danza Magnifico she had briefly forgotten the reason they were here in the first place. Her baby, her Storm, was somewhere here in Andalusia.

"You must want to rest now," Francoise was saying. "You have come such a long way. Perhaps you would like to take a siesta? We eat late here in Andalusia – dinner will be served at 10 p.m."

"No, Francoise," Issie said. "I know I should be tired, but I'm not."

Francoise smiled. "I understand. I am not either. I tell you what, why don't you have a shower and change into your jodhpurs? Meet me downstairs in ten minutes and I will take you on a tour of El Caballo and we can talk some more."

Ten minutes later, Issie came downstairs to find Francoise also freshly changed with her long black hair slicked back into a wet ponytail. She was wearing the traditional *vaquero* clothing of the Spanish cowboy – turned-up trousers with brown leather boots, a short cropped jacket known as a *chaquetilla*, and a wide-brimmed stockman's hat. Francoise handed Issie a hat too. "Put this on," she instructed. "The sun is hot here and you'll need it."

Francoise led the way back across the cobbled courtyard. At first Issie thought she was heading to the stables where the mares were, but then they kept walking past the mares' quarters, and Francoise took her past the fountain and through the archway that led to the stallions' loose boxes.

Issie had caught a glimpse of the mares' stables as they went past. They were in the old Spanish style, very traditional, stone stalls as dark and cool as catacombs. She had been expecting the stallions' quarters to be the same, but in fact they were quite different. On the outside they were classically Spanish too, but inside the loose boxes were all stainless steel and pale wood, sleek and ultra-modern.

"Roberto loves the history of El Caballo, but he is not always a traditionalist," Francoise explained as they walked down the row of stalls. "He rebuilt the stallions' quarters to match the best stables he visited when he was competing on the three-day event circuit in Europe."

Francoise reached one hand to the top half of the Dutch door on the first stall, slid the bolt and swung it open. There was a soft nicker from the stall and Marius appeared, craning his neck over the door to greet them.

"You know Marius, of course," Francoise said, reaching her hand up to stroke the nose of the grey stallion. Issie looked at Marius. Even though this horse was a fully grown stallion and Storm was still a colt, Issie could already see striking similarities between father and son. If she had ever had any doubts that Marius was Storm's sire, taking one look at the stallion made her absolutely certain that they shared the same blood. It was evident in the classical topline, the strong neck, shoulders and haunches. Marius was big for a Lipizzaner, almost sixteen-three hands high. Would Storm grow as big as his mighty sire? Would he look like this when he grew up?

Issie felt a shiver run through her. If she didn't find out who had stolen Storm, she might not have the chance to see him grow up at all.

Francoise grabbed a bridle off the hook behind her. "We only have Spanish saddles here, I hope that is OK?

They are quite different from the English ones, so I will show you how to tack up…"

Issie was confused. "We're going riding? I thought we were just taking a tour of El Caballo."

"We are!" Francoise responded brightly. "Did you think I was just showing you around the stables? I meant a tour of the land itself. And for that…" she said as she walked over to the next loose box, "… you will need a horse."

Francoise stood in front of the loose box and made a clucking sound with her tongue. "Come on, Angel," she said, softly coaxing. "It's OK, boy, it's me. I've brought someone to meet you." At the sound of Francoise's voice, the horse at the back of the stall gave a nicker and stepped forward into the light, thrusting his magnificent head out over the Dutch door.

He was a stallion, almost as big as Marius, and so handsome! Issie stared up at him. His face had the elegance of a classical Andalusian, with wide-set, soulful eyes and a dark, sooty muzzle. Unlike Marius, who still had grey dapples, this stallion's coat was absolutely white, as pure as parchment. His mane tumbled over his neck and shoulders, lustrous and pearly, like the foaming white crest of a wave.

The great beauty of this horse made it all the more

upsetting for Issie when she saw the scars. On the bridge of the stallion's nose, just where the noseband would normally sit, was a series of jagged gashes that had healed to form ugly scar tissue. The scars must have been caused by deep cuts into the stallion's flesh. The wounds were so profound they had left these heartbreaking marks as a legacy, destroying the stallion's otherwise perfect beauty.

Issie reached out a hand and touched the stallion's muzzle. He gave a soft nicker as she gently stroked his noble face, her hand running over the bumps and lumps, as if she were reading them like Braille beneath her fingers.

"How did he get these?" Issie asked Francoise.

"They were part of his training," Francoise said quietly. Issie was shocked.

"No, no," Francoise shook her head. "Not here. Please understand, Isadora, we did not do this to Angel. It was a rival stable. The hacienda of Miguel Vega. Vega is a great horseman – but a cruel one too. In Spain, there is a special noseband called a *serreta*. The *serreta* has sharp metal teeth that dig into the bridge of the horse's nose until he submits. It is very cruel. Throughout Spain, the *serreta* is considered an instrument of torture and is now banned. However, some horsemen, including Vega, continue to use them, even though it causes the horses unbelievable pain."

Issie ran her hand over Angel's scars once more. "So the *serreta* did this to Angel?"

"Miguel Vega did it to him," Francoise said angrily. "Angel once belonged to him. Vega put the *serreta* on him when he was less than a year old – to break his spirit."

"But if he's Vega's horse, then what is he doing here?" Issie asked.

"The race for the Silver Bridle," Francoise explained. "The winning stable gets to take five horses of their choosing from each of their rivals." Francoise reached out a hand to stroke Angel's silver mane. "When we won against Vega's stable ten years ago, I had just joined El Caballo. I was given the chance to choose a horse myself – and I chose Angel."

"I can see why," Issie said softly. "He's very beautiful."

"*Oui,*" Francoise agreed. "But that is not why I chose him. I picked him because of his speed. Angel's bloodlines date back to some of the greatest racehorses in the history of Spain. His sire has won many, many races. And I knew Angel could be fast too. I thought that one day, when he was fully grown, he would be able to defend El Caballo Danza Magnifico against Vega's stables. He would race for us and bring home the Silver Bridle."

"So will he be racing this time," Issie asked, "against the other stables?"

Francoise shook her head. "I do not think so. Roberto wants Alfonso to ride for us in the race. A jockey needs to be light and quick and Alfie is the best in our stables."

"Well, why doesn't Alfonso ride Angel?" Issie was confused.

"Because Angel will not allow it," Francoise said. "Ever since Vega put the *serreta* on him Angel has been afraid of men. He trembles at their touch. He will not allow a male jockey on his back. He has thrown all of our best riders – including Alfie. Of course," Francoise added cheekily, "I'm sure you'll be fine."

"What!" Issie couldn't believe it. "You're joking, right? You don't really expect me to ride him? He'll throw me too!"

"You are not a man, are you?" Francoise smiled. "Angel has never thrown me. He will not throw you. It is only men that he fears, and rightly so, for it was a man – a brutal and cruel man – who did this to him."

"Poor Angel." Issie looked at the stallion's gentle face, those soulful black eyes. "Anyone who could hurt a horse like this must be a monster."

Francoise suddenly went very quiet and didn't respond.

"The brushes are in the stall," she said, changing the subject. "You can groom him while I fetch the saddles."

Grooming Angel proved to be quite different from brushing Blaze or Comet. For starters, the grey stallion was much taller than her horses at home. Issie tried tiptoeing at first and then had to give up and turn the grooming bucket upside down to stand on it so she could reach his mane. It usually took Issie no time at all to whip a comb through Blaze's mane, which was kept pulled short and neat, but Angel's mane was quite different. It was long and silky, like fairy-tale princess hair.

"Aren't you beautiful?" Issie said under her breath as she ran her body brush along the crest of Angel's magnificent neck. Then she caught sight of those scars once more and a shiver ran up her spine.

"Here you go!" Francoise's voice startled her back to reality. She passed Angel's bridle over to her and Issie was shocked when she saw that there were long black leather tassels hanging down the front of the brow band.

Francoise smiled. "Don't worry, it is not a *serreta*. That's just a *mosqueto*, a fly switch – all the horses here wear them."

Issie put on the bridle and then Francoise showed her how to put on the Spanish *vaquero* saddle. It was heavy, and twice the size of Issie's normal saddle, with a sheepskin pad on the top of it.

"It's like sitting in an armchair!" Issie giggled when Francoise legged her up.

Francoise led the two horses out into the courtyard and then mounted Marius. She smiled at Issie. "Have you ridden a stallion before?" she asked.

Issie nodded. "My Aunt Hester has a black warmblood called Destiny."

"Spanish stallions are quite different, you will see," Francoise said. "Angel has a temperament that matches his name. He is a sweetheart. I ride him all the time and he is very fit. Although," she added, "he may be a little fresh. I have not ridden him for two weeks."

Angel was indeed fresh. The stallion fought against Issie's grasp as they rode out into the courtyard, cantering on the spot with eagerness as she held him back.

"Follow me!" Francoise called over her shoulder as she pressed Marius on into a canter and set off across the courtyard towards the wrought-iron gates at the entrance of the hacienda. Issie followed, but she was still holding Angel back to a trot, afraid of the speed the stallion had in him.

Angel was sixteen-two, the same height as Destiny,

but he was much more muscular, with a broad neck and powerful haunches typical of his Spanish breed. Issie could feel the incredible strength this horse possessed, and it scared her. What would happen if she let the stallion get his head? She gripped the reins tight in her fists as they cantered out of the gates, holding Angel back as they trailed behind Marius.

"Are you OK?" Francoise looked back over her shoulder as she cantered on.

"Uh-huh," Issie nodded. She was still holding Angel back tightly.

"Let him have his head a little," Francoise said. "You can trust him."

Issie realised at that moment how she must look up there on Angel's back, her mouth held rigid with fear, hands stiff with nervous tension. She took a deep breath and did as Francoise said, relaxing her shoulders, softening her hands and releasing the reins a little. She was amazed when Angel didn't suddenly bolt off. He relaxed too and fell into a steady stride alongside Marius.

"Good boy!" Issie gave him a slappy pat. She sat up in the saddle and looked around her, beginning to enjoy the ride, taking in the beauty of the El Caballo estate. It was beyond gorgeous here, the fields full of mares and their foals, grazing or sheltering from the heat under the low-hanging boughs of the olive trees.

They cantered on, heading towards the rocky foothills at the rear of the estate, and as the ground underfoot began to get rocky Francoise pulled Marius up to a trot. "The footing is rough from here on," she said. Then she pointed at the hills ahead where bare, grey boulders marked the entrance to a narrow gorge. "We go through here," she said. "Follow me. It gets very narrow at certain points, only wide enough for us to ride in single file, but do not worry, the horses know this path well. It leads to the higher pasture, El Caballo land where the mares and stallions graze when grass is scarce during the dry months."

Francoise clucked Marius on and Issie followed behind. The sheepskin saddle was so comfy she tried riding a sitting trot instead of rising up and down and found it to be quite easy. Angel's trot was floaty, which helped a lot. She was already getting a feel for the stallion's paces, and she was sure that the horse was beginning to understand her aids too, listening to her cues. She could see Angel's ears swivelling back and forth, a sign that he was paying attention to her, as they negotiated their way through the gorge.

Not that Angel had any choice but to keep moving straight ahead. The gorge was narrow, with sheer rockface rising high on either side. Nothing grew here in the pale chalky soil except for a few tufts of tussock sticking out of the cliffs. Issie looked up and saw the gap between the cliffs above her and a thin river of blue sky floating over her head. Then she lowered her eyes to the front once more, her gaze set on Francoise's back as they rode on.

"It is not much further to the other side," Francoise called over her shoulder, anticipating Issie's question. And then, a few moments later, the narrow path became wider again and they were clear of the gorge and out the other side once more with flat, dry pasture stretching out in front of them.

Francoise pulled Marius to a halt. "This is the high pasture, the last of El Caballo grazing lands," she explained to Issie. She pointed ahead of her. "Do you see that orange grove and the brick wall with the turrets beyond the trees?"

Issie nodded.

"That is Miguel Vega's hacienda," Francoise said. "The orange trees mark the point where our land stops and his property begins." Francoise's eyes narrowed against the sun as she stared ahead. "It is only natural, I suppose, that the two best horse studs in Spain should be right beside each other like this," she said. "Vega's family has been here for centuries, just like Roberto's. Their ancestors knew that this lush, fertile land was the best place to raise horses. And it was only natural too, I suppose, that the families would become such great rivals."

Issie reached a hand down to stroke Angel's neck and, as she did so, she caught a glimpse of the stallion's profile and the ugly scars that marred his beautiful face. "I hope I never meet Miguel Vega," Issie said. "If he could do this to Angel then he must be horrible."

Francoise looked tense. "Isadora, I am very much afraid that you may have to meet him." She took a deep breath before the words came stumbling out. "Because we think it is Miguel Vega who has taken Nightstorm."

Chapter 7

Issie would have ridden to Vega's straight away to confront him and demand that he return the colt if Francoise hadn't grabbed at Angel's reins and held her back, calming her down until she saw sense.

"It is useless to go in there angry and without any plan," she said bluntly. "If you really want to get Storm back then we must be smart about it. Miguel Vega went to great lengths to steal your colt – do you really think he will simply hand him back again?"

Even in her fury, Issie had the sense to listen to Francoise. "I should never have brought you here like this," Francoise said. "I am sorry. I know it is hard, but please be patient, now is not the time. You will only endanger your colt if you rush off to face Vega now."

And so Issie cast one last, longing look at Vega's hacienda, and then turned Angel around under Francoise's watchful eye and followed Marius back into the gorge towards El Caballo Danza Magnifico.

She knew Francoise was right. Yet at that moment, turning her back on her colt had been unbearable. To be so near, and still unable to help him, was beyond painful. Francoise reassured her that it wouldn't be long to wait.

"We will get our chance tomorrow – at the *feria*. It is a huge festival, held every ten years to celebrate the race for the Silver Bridle. Vega is bound to be there. Roberto will tell you all about it when we meet for dinner tonight."

Dinner that evening was held in the main dining room and was a grand affair to celebrate the arrival of the guests. Issie hadn't been sure if she would like Spanish food, but everything tasted wonderful – there was deep fried calamari, fresh tomato bread and rich, hearty paella.

Alfonso had clearly been expecting to spend the meal talking to Avery about the good old days and his father's adventures, but Avery fobbed him off.

"I don't know what tall stories your father has told you

about me," Avery grinned, "but that was a long time ago. These days I lead a very quiet life."

"It doesn't sound very exciting," Alfonso said. "Who would give up international eventing to be head instructor at a pony club?"

"Alfie!" Roberto told him off.

"No," Avery said, "I know what he means. When I gave up riding, I had offers of all kinds of jobs, which I suppose you would call glamorous, but I wanted to do something that really helped young riders." He cast a glance at Issie. "Besides, a lot more action happens in Chevalier Point than you might think."

It was Roberto who brought the conversation around to Miguel Vega. As he told everyone at the table about what a monster Vega was and his fears that it was Vega who had taken the colt, Issie and Francoise exchanged looks. Issie wanted to blurt out the news about their ride today to Vega's hacienda, but it was clear from the swift kick that Francoise delivered under the table that it would be best not to mention it. Instead, she remained quiet as Roberto explained about tomorrow's *feria*.

"The parade is a great tradition, a chance for the haciendas to celebrate and show off their best horses before the race the following weekend," he explained.

"I would be honoured if you would both ride alongside us as guests of El Caballo Danza Magnifico."

"So all of the twelve haciendas will be there?" Avery asked. "Including Vega's?"

"*Oui*," Francoise answered him. "Especially Vega's. He would not miss this chance to boast – he expects to win this year. He will be there, riding his best stallion, the black giant Victorioso, the horse that he will ride in the race."

"Vega doesn't have a jockey from his stables who can ride for him?" Avery asked.

"Pah!" Roberto snorted. "Vega is too vain. The tubby old fool believes he is the best horse rider – the only one at his stables who is good enough to ride in the Silver Bridle."

"The rival haciendas assemble in the village square," Francoise continued. "The parade starts at the entrance to the square and follows along the same route where the race will take place."

"I don't understand." Issie was confused. "How can the race take place in the middle of a village square?"

"Isadora," Francoise said, "the Silver Bridle is no ordinary horse race. It is not run on a race track the way your thoroughbreds race in New Zealand. The race is meant to test not only the speed of the horse, but also the courage of the rider, and for this reason the race is run through the very streets of the village, the same way that our ancestors rode it two hundred years ago when the tradition began."

"On the street?" Issie couldn't believe it. She imagined horses running through the narrow dusty alleyways of the Spanish villages she had driven through on her way to El Caballo Danza Magnifico. "That would be suicide!" Issie shook her head.

"It is very dangerous," Francoise agreed. "The village square itself is quite wide, but not wide enough for twelve horses, as you can imagine. There is much shoving and pushing from the riders, and from the crowds who line the streets and cheer for each hacienda."

"How far do the horses run?" Avery asked.

"Three times around the square. Almost two kilometres – the same length as a normal horse race," Francoise said. "But not all of them will make it to the finish line. The course is dangerous and the jockeys are ruthless. They will fight tooth and nail to get a clear space as they gallop and there are always dirty tactics. Every time this race has been run, a horse has fallen. Many have been injured or even died in the course of this race."

"Why don't you just tell them you won't take part in the race? Can't you just say no?"

Alfonso shook his head. "You do not understand how deep this tradition is with us, Isadora. To win the Silver Bridle demands the utmost skill, the greatest courage. It is a test of true manliness. To refuse to race would be the mark of a coward."

"So you'll risk your best horse?" Issie was horrified. "You'll risk Marius, just to prove that you are a man?"

"Do not misunderstand my son," Roberto said. "We do not take this lightly. Yes, there are risks, for Marius, and for Alfonso also. But it is the way of our people, our tradition and our culture. I cannot turn my back on it, and neither can Alfonso. No matter what happens, El Caballo Danza Magnifico will take part in this race, just as we have done now for nearly two centuries."

"Don't you see, Issie?" Francoise looked at her pleadingly. "This is a good thing. If Alfie and Marius win the race, if El Caballo takes the Silver Bridle, then we get to choose five horses from every stable."

"So?" Issie said.

Francoise reached and grasped Issie's hand in her own. "So if we win, we can choose Nightstorm as one of the five. We can get the colt back."

Issie had never expected Roberto Nunez's hacienda to have email access. The traditional Andalusian stone villa was over two centuries old. The very last thing Issie had expected to stumble across was a hi-tech media room.

Issie had found the room by mistake before dinner that evening. She had walked in, thinking it must be the bathroom, and had been confronted by computer screens and electronic gadgets. Francoise had laughed at Issie's amazement when she spoke about it at dinner that night. "El Caballo Danza Magnifico performs around the world. We're a big international business, so naturally we are very well-equipped here."

After dinner, Francoise lent Issie one of the laptop computers from the office. "It is wireless, so you can access the internet and your emails from anywhere in the house, including your room," she explained.

The first person Issie emailed of course was Stella. It was an enormous long email all about everything that had happened so far. Issie told Stella about the shock of discovering that Avery and Roberto were old friends. She described in detail how beautiful and exotic the surroundings were at the hacienda. She wrote about riding Angel for the first time and Francoise's suspicions that Vega was the one responsible for taking Storm.

Stella emailed back immediately and her email was just one line.

Ohmygod! she wrote, **Alfonso sounds really dishy. Is he handsome? I bet he is! He probably looks just like one of the Jonas Brothers!**

Issie groaned when she read it. Typical boy-mad Stella!

Alfonso is really nice, Issie wrote back, **and yes, I suppose he is handsome. But in case you'd forgotten, Stella, I already have a boyfriend – his name is Aidan!**

Issie hadn't forgotten about Aidan. She thought about him all the time, even if she hadn't seen him for months since she left Blackthorn Farm. Aidan had sent her a few emails since then. He had written to say that the film job, the one that had previously fallen through, was now back on and they were back in the movie business. He and Aunt Hester had loads of well-paid work and the farm was now financially secure.

She was about to start on an email to Aidan when there was a knock at the door and Avery came in.

"Francoise told me you were doing some emailing," Avery said. "I just wanted to remind you to write one to your mum. I promised her that you would let her know once you'd arrived safely."

"OK," Issie replied. She stifled a yawn. What was the time, anyway? She looked at the clock over her bed. "Wow. It's nearly midnight." She was surprised.

"They stay up late in Spain," Avery said. "We'll have to get used to their timetable. They eat dinner at ten, they go to sleep at midnight and they have siestas in the afternoons. The whole place stops for a nap at three o'clock."

"Even the grown-ups?" Issie was amazed by this. "How long do they sleep for?"

"A couple of hours," Avery said. "They do it because it's too hot in the afternoons to do any work. It's the tradition here."

"Yeah, there are lots of weird traditions here," Issie said darkly.

Avery looked at her. "You mean the Silver Bridle?"

Issie nodded. "Tom, I just don't get it. Storm is my colt. Why do we have to wait to run some stupid race to win him back? Why don't we just go to Vega's stables and force him to give Storm to us?"

"I think we have to trust Roberto on this one," Avery said to her. "He knows the culture here and if he says the race is our best chance to get Nightstorm back from Vega, we have to go along with him."

Issie wasn't sure about this, but she was too tired to argue. "I'm gonna email Mum and then go to bed," she told Avery.

"Good idea," her instructor said. "Get some sleep. It's a big day tomorrow."

Chapter 8

Preparations for the *feria* took the entire morning. Saddles were polished until they glistened and every rider in El Caballo stables put on their best *vaquero* costume. It was the horses, though, who got the most attention. Their coats were groomed until they shone and their manes were plaited, not in the traditional English way seen at gymkhanas, but with thick double-rows of French plaits that ran in two braids down each side of the horse's neck from one end of the mane to the other. Their tails too, were dressed, the top halves plaited into a long French braid and then the switch of the tail elaborately knotted up at the end.

Issie was riding Angel again for the parade and had saddled him herself that morning with a rainbow saddle cloth for the occasion. The stable grooms had helped her get ready too, showing her the Spanish way of tying brilliantly coloured red, orange and violet bobbles into the stallion's mane.

By eleven o'clock all the riders were mounted and ready to go. Except for Francoise.

"What is taking her so long?" Avery checked his watch.

"Here she is!" Issie said.

Francoise emerged into the cobbled courtyard, not in her usual uniform of *vaquero* trousers and jacket, but in a hot-pink flamenco dress covered with large black polka dots. The dress hugged tight to Francoise's body all the way down past her hips and then turned into a riot of frills and flounces around her legs. She wore her hair tied back severely in a bun, with a gigantic red rose securing it in place.

"It is traditional." Francoise shrugged when Issie and Avery both stared at her wide-eyed as she walked over to join them, taking the reins of her mare. "Although I cannot say I am happy about having to ride side-saddle in this dress," she added grumpily. "One cannot control a horse properly riding side-saddle."

Francoise had chosen one of El Caballo's chestnut Anglo-Arab mares to ride to the *feria* today. Issie was riding alongside her, Roberto was riding Marius, and Avery had been given one of Roberto's best stallions, a bay Lusitano called Sorcerer. Six other *vaqueros*, including Alfonso, were also riding with them today, each of them on one of El Caballo's grey Lipizzaner stallions.

As the riders headed out through the gates of the hacienda they instantly fell into groups. Avery and Roberto rode ahead together laughing and chatting, at ease with each other as only old friends can be. Alfonso rode out at the front of them alone, holding the El Caballo flag. Behind all of them rode the El Caballo horsemen, and then Issie and Francoise, bringing up the rear. Apart from Francoise, who was riding a mare, Issie noticed that all of the other riders had something in common.

"Why does no one ride geldings here?" Issie asked Francoise as they trotted out of the El Caballo gates, heading up the dusty hillside road that would lead them the short distance to the village.

"In Spain it is only stallions," Francoise explained. "The Spanish stallion is not as wild and uncontrollable as other breeds. Indeed he is so well-mannered that even small children of three or four years old can be seen riding a stallion."

Francoise looked over at Issie's horse. "Angel is such

a typical Andalusian stallion," she said. "I remember when we first brought him to El Caballo as a young colt. He had been so badly mistreated by Vega and he was terrified of men, but even then he would always let me near him, and his nature was so gentle, so sweet. He is nearly eleven now, but he has not changed. Whenever I am home at El Caballo, I ride him each day and I marvel at how willing he is. He will do anything for you. You will see."

Issie knew what Francoise meant. When she had ridden Destiny there was always the sense of a power struggle between her and the black stallion. He was wilful, with a mind of his own. Angel wasn't like that at all – he was sensitive and willing to please. It made Issie even sadder about the scars on Angel's nose. Why would Vega use a barbed metal noseband on such a sweet-natured horse as this? It didn't make sense.

The village was on the hill rising up above El Caballo Danza Magnifico. It was a pretty sight with its whitewashed terraced houses with terracotta roofs all built right next door to each other. The houses all clustered around the central square, which was where Issie and the other riders were heading. They trotted their horses up the winding cobbled streets and gathered at the entrance to the square, where the other riders were organising themselves into their haciendas, preparing to parade under their racing colours around the fountain at the centre of the square.

Issie realised now that the red, orange and violet bobbles tied in Angel's mane were not purely for decoration – they denoted the colour of El Caballo Danza Magnifico's hacienda. As each of the twelve haciendas assembled by the entrance to the square their flag bearer rode to the front so that the other riders representing his stables could line up behind him. Each flag bearer held aloft the colourful banner that bore their hacienda insignia. El Caballo's flag was golden and in the middle was a red letter C with the red heart stamped inside it. Carrying the flag, Alfonso rode to the front of the El Caballo riders, smiling at Issie as he cantered past her.

"Look!" Francoise said to Issie. "It is so high up here, you can see all the way back to El Caballo. The hacienda looks beautiful, doesn't it?"

Issie looked across the square. Francoise was right, you could see the house and stables quite clearly from here. At the gates she could make out an El Caballo flag, the same as the one that Alfonso was carrying, fluttering in the wind on the flagpole.

There was a mood of anticipation now, as the flag bearers shouted out to their riders as last-minute preparations began. Issie wanted to get excited too, to get into the spirit of the *feria*, but she couldn't. She was still so desperately worried about Nightstorm. She hadn't really been concentrating when the flag bearers explained what to do, and she couldn't speak Spanish anyway. She suddenly felt overwhelmed and bewildered.

"It's OK. Stick with me," Francoise told her. She pulled her Anglo-Arab up to ride alongside Issie. "All we must do is ride once around the square so that everyone can admire our horses." And then she added under her breath, "Of course, this admiration comes at a price. Most of the haciendas are here trying to decide which horses they will claim from their rival stables if they are lucky enough to win the race."

Which horse would Issie choose if she won? The truth was, as she looked around at the stallions, mares, fillies and colts being paraded in the *feria*, Issie would have chosen all of them. Each horse seemed more beautiful than the next. And then, one particular horse caught her eye. He was a gigantic jet-black stallion, enormous, almost seventeen hands high, and solid with it. Unlike the other stallions in the parade, who all seemed to share the placid

Spanish nature, this black stallion had fire in his belly. He skipped and danced beneath his master as they rode back and forth. While the other riders in the parade marched obediently behind the flag bearer, the man on the black stallion paid no attention and rode ahead, circling his flag bearer and horses like a shark. Issie looked at the flag, which was bright yellow and black with a capital V surrounded by curlicues on either side ϛVϛ.

"Which hacienda is that?" Issie asked, pointing it out to Francoise.

Francoise didn't have the chance to answer Issie's question before a string of young horses came into view behind the yellow and black flag. The young horses were riderless, a string of colts and fillies, all wearing neck collars that joined together with leashes so that the line of horses formed a cobra.

Leading the cobra was a man on a grey stallion with a stock whip. He kept the young horses in line behind the man who carried the yellow and black flag. There were four colts in the cobra. The first three colts were almost identical, all of them steel-grey, with the classical physique of the Spanish Andalusian. But the fourth colt was quite different. He was a bay, with a broad white blaze and an elegant dished face with pretty wide-set eyes. Issie saw him and her heart leapt.

"Storm!" she called out across the square.

Before anyone could stop her, she had turned Angel and was barging her way back through the crowded parade, going against the tide, pushing past the other horses and riders. She could no longer see Storm, he was lost in the crowd now, but she kept her eyes on the yellow and black flag that marked the spot where her colt must be.

"Storm!!"

There was no way the colt could possibly hear Issie's cries over the noise of the parade. Was she even getting closer to him? It was hard enough to hold her ground against the crowds who were pushing past her, going in the opposite direction. She kept losing sight of the yellow and black flag. Where was Storm?

Panic-stricken, she pulled Angel to a halt, took a deep breath and gave two short, sharp whistles – the same signal she used to call Storm in the paddock at home.

The bay colt heard her call and he returned it with a heartfelt whinny, letting her know that he was there.

"Storm!" Issie kicked Angel on again, heading in the direction of the colt's cry, forcing her way on through the crowd. Behind her, Alfonso had been the first one to realise what was going on. He had turned too and was trying to follow her through the parade, but his flag was making it hard to manoeuvre. Francoise was right behind him, making apologies to people as they barged through the crowd, pushing past the other riders as she tried to catch up.

There was a brief moment when the procession suddenly swelled around her and Issie lost Storm once more in a blur of horses and colourful flags – and then she urged Angel on and suddenly they were through and on the other side of the parade. The crowds had cleared and Issie was sitting there on Angel, staring directly at the man who held the cobra of colts.

"Hey!" Issie shouted at the man. "Where did you get him from? That's my colt!"

The man, who clearly didn't speak English, looked at her blankly as she pointed at Storm.

"You have my horse," Issie repeated slowly, "and I want him back."

The man shrugged at her and then turned away and shouted something in Spanish that Issie didn't understand. A moment later, the ranks of riders wearing the yellow and black colours of the hacienda opened up to let through the man on the gigantic black stallion, the one that Issie had first noticed in the crowd.

Now that she was closer Issie could see that although the horse was large, the man was not. He was short, and far too fat for the traditional *vaquero* costume that he was wearing. His gut bulged over the black satin cummerbund of his trousers. Underneath his black oiled hair, beads of sweat kept forming on his forehead and he dabbed at these with a white handkerchief. His eyes were beady and small, his face dominated by a very thick, bushy moustache.

"Hey *chica*! Little girl! What's going on?" the man on the stallion mocked her. "Do you not understand Spanish or do you think you are being funny? You're blocking our way. The parade has begun. Get a move on!"

Issie didn't move. "You have my colt," she said. "That bay colt there – he's mine and I want him back."

"You cannot make a claim on the property of Miguel Vega!" the man said dismissively.

"Miguel Vega is nothing but a thief," Issie said, shaking with fury, "and I'm not making a claim. I'm telling you. That colt does not belong to Vega – his name is Nightstorm and he is mine."

As Issie said this, Alfonso finally reached her side. "Are you OK?" He looked at Issie. She shook her head. "Alfonso, that's him. That's my colt. He's got Storm."

Alfonso turned to face the man on the black stallion.

"You've got a nerve stealing that colt and then bringing him here, Miguel."

Miguel? Issie suddenly clicked. Of course! This man in front of them was none other than Vega himself!

Francoise had joined them now. She had a steely look in her eyes as she rode past Issie and Alfonso, taking up position in front of them to confront the grinning man with the moustache.

"Miguel. You've gone too far this time. You know that the colt belongs to this girl and she has nothing to do with our feud, or the race. Why don't we settle this now? Do the right thing and give him back."

Vega gave a smirk at this. "You're mistaken, Francoise. The colt is one of ours. Look at the brand!"

Issie looked down at Nightstorm and as the colt danced about, fighting against his handlers, she caught a glimpse of his hindquarters. Freshly burned into his left haunch was the ~V~ brand of the Vega stables.

Vega sneered at Francoise. "You see? You insult Miguel Vega! I do not need to steal your feeble horses! I will win the five best horses in your stable anyway when Victorioso and I cross the line ahead of you for the Silver Bridle!"

All this time, as they had been standing there facing Vega, Issie had been struggling to control Angel. The stallion had been pacing and fretting beneath her, fighting her hands, desperate to get away from the man with the moustache. It hadn't occurred to Issie until now that Angel would have a lingering memory of Vega's cruelty, and that the stallion would be so terrified of his former master. She was struggling to keep him still so that she could confront Vega. "Steady, boy," Issie breathed, trying to hold the stallion as he danced beneath her.

"Ah!" Vega said. "I see you are riding Angel. He still bears the marks of my *serreta*." He laughed and reached out a hand to touch the stallion's scarred face. Angel instantly pulled back and Issie struggled once more to hang on to the reins and control him.

Vega laughed again and looked at Storm. "We shall soon see how this little one likes the *serreta*. He is almost old enough, I think, to begin his training."

"You leave him alone!" Issie shouted. Before she could stop to think about it she had kicked Angel on and was aiming her horse straight at Vega, her hand raised, ready to strike at the man with her closed fist.

"Hah!" Vega reached out his own hand and caught Issie's arm in midair, grasping her wrist tightly. "We have a young wildcat here! You need to control your child, Francoise! I might need to use the *serreta* on her as well."

"Let go of her!" Francoise egged her horse on, riding forward to reach out her hand and free Issie from Vega's grasp. As she did so, though, Vega's enormous black stallion reared up. Vega had no choice but to let go of Issie's wrist as the horse rose up underneath him. But Francoise was still riding forward to help her and as the big, black stallion came back down to the ground his front hoof caught a glancing blow on Francoise's shoulder.

Francoise let out a scream of pain and toppled forward from her side-saddle to land hard on the ground. Then her chestnut mare reared up in fright and suddenly there were horses loose everywhere and riders yelling and shouting in panic, jostling and shoving each other to try and get clear.

"Francoise!" Issie was trying to find the Frenchwoman, but she was out of sight on the ground, in danger of being trampled in the blur of hooves.

Alfonso fought the crowds too, struggling to reach Francoise, but it was Avery who appeared out of nowhere and managed to reach her in time. Realising the danger to anyone who was dismounted among the rabble of panicked horses, he stayed on his horse and reached down low to grab Francoise by the arm. Yanking her roughly to her feet, he grabbed her tight and threw her across the saddle in front of him. Francoise was clearly in pain, and had to use all her strength to cling on desperately as Avery rode to get them clear of the crowds.

"I've got her." Avery lifted Francoise to safety. "Issie! Follow us!" But Issie was already heading in the opposite direction, fighting her way back into the crowd to look for Storm. Vega's riders had all disappeared in the fracas and the colt was nowhere to be seen. She rode into the crowd, being barged and shoved by other horses and riders as she tried to force her way through to the last place she had seen Vega and her colt.

"Come on!" She felt a hand on her shoulder. It was Alfonso. "It's no use, Issie," Alfonso insisted. "Vega is arrogant, but he's not stupid. He knows better than to hang around after that. You won't find him now. He's already gone and he's taken Storm with him."

Issie ignored Alfonso. She kept looking, her eyes searching out the bay colt, hoping to catch a glimpse of Storm in the crowd of horses and riders.

"You'll get hurt if you stay in the way here," Alfonso said. "Come on, please. Follow me."

Alfonso led Issie and Angel out of the crowd, past the crush of horses and riders to a clear space where a row of park benches lined the far side of the town square.

There they found Avery, bent over Francoise who was lying very still on one of the benches, her breathing harsh and laboured.

"Is she OK?" Issie said, as she slid off Angel and ran to join them.

"It's my arm," Francoise said, gritting her teeth through the pain. "I think it's broken." She tried to sit up. "Did you get Storm? Where is he?"

Issie shook her head. "I don't know. Vega had him, he must have—" She couldn't finish her sentence. She couldn't bring herself to admit that her colt had been right there and they had lost him again. They had missed their chance to save the colt. Storm was gone.

Chapter 9

Back at El Caballo that afternoon the mood was dark. Francoise's arm was indeed broken. Alfonso had driven her to the hospital in Seville where they had X-rayed her and put the arm in a plaster cast before releasing her home again. Now she lay on the floral brocade sofa in the living room, with Avery and Issie fussing over her, plumping her cushions and bringing her fresh orange juice and pills to dull the pain.

"This is all my fault," Issie said. "I'm so sorry, Francoise. I shouldn't have lost my temper when Vega said he was going to use the *serreta* on Storm…"

"It is OK, really." Francoise smiled. "I do not blame you – it was this stupid flamenco costume!" She smoothed down the ruffles of her dress with obvious irritation.

"I could not stay on when the horse reared, with that ridiculous side-saddle and all these silly frills! Next time I shall wear my *vaquero* trousers!"

"I agree. Flamenco dresses are not appropriate attire for fighting on horseback," Roberto Nunez said sarcastically, as he entered the room carrying a tray laden with tea and cakes. He put the tray down on the coffee table in front of them and shook his head in disbelief. "I turn my back for a moment and what happens? When I turn round again I see all four of you at the other end of the village square, caught up in a fight with Vega! What were you thinking? Did you think Vega would just give the colt back? Alfonso? Francoise? You both know him better than that!"

"But Dad," Alfonso objected. "You weren't there. You didn't see Vega, the way he spoke to Isadora. He was so arrogant—"

Roberto cut his son off with a harsh look. "His arrogance will lose him the Silver Bridle, but only if we keep our heads. I expect my son to beat him in the race, not in a street fight."

Alfonso looked as if he was going to argue back, but Roberto waved away his objections with a brisk hand. "Go down to the stables and check on the horses," he instructed. "Make sure that none of them were hurt."

Alfonso looked annoyed, but he didn't argue. He nodded to his father and left the room.

"Well, one good thing has come of this," Roberto sighed. "At least we know for certain now that Vega has the colt."

"Does that mean we can call the police?" Issie asked.

Roberto shook his head. "I wish that were the case, but we still have no proof that the colt is yours," he said. "Vega has branded it with the mark of his stables – if anything, the colt now appears to be even more his property than he was before."

"But Storm isn't his!" Issie looked pleadingly at Avery. "Tom, we have to do something. I can't leave Storm with Vega."

"Issie, Roberto is right," Avery said. "Vega currently holds all the cards. If we go to the police now they won't believe us. It's our word against his. We must wait until the time is right…"

"When?" Issie said. "When will that be? After Vega has used the *serreta* on him, the same way he did to Angel? That man is a monster – and he's got my colt!"

"Isadora," Roberto cautioned, "I know how much you love your colt, but your impetuousness today has already got us into trouble. Now I must ask you to wait. Let us decide what to do."

"I'm sorry…" Issie was taken aback. "I wasn't trying to cause trouble… I didn't mean for anyone to get hurt…"

"I know that," Roberto said gently. "But for your own safety, Isadora, please, let us handle this. I do not want to see anything happen to you."

Issie looked around the room at Francoise and Avery. They were both silent, which Issie took as a sign that they were in agreement with Roberto.

She felt hot tears pricking at her eyes. *Great*, she thought, *now it's all my fault, and to make it worse I'm going to start crying like a kid in front of everyone.* "You know," she said, trying to focus on the plate of cakes in front of her as the tears blurred her vision, "I'm not very hungry right now. I think I'm going to go to my room for a while."

Issie left the living room, shutting the door behind her. She stood outside, pausing for a moment. What was she going to do now? Roberto had made it clear that he thought fighting to get Storm back was futile, and Avery and Francoise seemed to agree with him. Still, did they really expect Issie to sit back and do nothing while Vega had her colt?

What else could she do, though? Issie was halfway around the world, without her friends or her family. If she was home then she could rely on Mystic turning up to help her. But here, in Spain? She was on her own. In fact, she had never felt more alone in her entire life.

Issie slumped back against the cool stone wall of the hallway just outside the living room door. She let herself slide down the wall until she was sitting on the floor with her arms wrapped around her knees. She couldn't just stay here at the hacienda and do nothing!

She reached a hand to her throat and felt for her necklace. It was a friendship necklace, the sort where the heart splits in two and you keep one half and give the other half to your best friend. Francoise had given her this necklace. Issie wore her half of the gold heart on a gold chain around her neck. The other half of the heart was attached to Blaze's halter. Issie never took the necklace off. She liked to reach up and touch it sometimes, to remind her that no matter where she was, her heart was always with her mare, back in Chevalier Point.

Issie shook her head. That was what Roberto didn't understand. Storm wasn't just any colt, he was Blaze's son. She loved him with the same passion that she loved Blaze. And now Storm needed her. She wasn't going to let him down.

Filled with determination, Issie was about to push

herself back up off the floor and head up the stairs to her room when she heard voices coming from the living room. It sounded like they were arguing. She could hear Francoise complaining, "Your honour is all very well and good, but Miguel plays dirty."

Then she heard Roberto snap back. "I don't want my hacienda seen brawling with a common horse thief like Vega." Then suddenly the door swung open and Francoise D'arth came stomping out. She strode straight past Issie, muttering something to herself in French. She was heading straight for the kitchen and didn't cast a backwards glance, so she didn't see the girl crouched on the other side of the door frame, even though she swept so close to her that Issie felt the flounces of her flamenco dress as she breezed past. Francoise had left the living-room door open behind her, and this meant that Issie could hear Roberto and Avery's conversation. They were speaking to each other very seriously.

"*Madre Mia*, my friend!" Roberto said. "No one will listen to me today!"

"They're just trying to help. You know that, Roberto," Avery said.

"I know, I know," Roberto sighed, "but they underestimate Vega. Thomas, the man is a fat fool, but he is still dangerous. I don't want them to get involved with him and get hurt. You can see that, can't you?"

"What about the race?" Avery countered. "Couldn't Alfie get hurt then?"

"That is different," Roberto said. "The race is our tradition. It is the right way to win your colt."

"Issie just wants her horse back," Avery said. "She doesn't care about tradition."

"You must watch her closely," Roberto warned him. "She must stay away from Vega."

"I think you've made that clear to her," Avery said, "but yes, of course I'll keep an eye on her. You mustn't be too tough on her though, Roberto. She's in love with that colt."

"She is impetuous and too spirited…"

"… just like we were at her age," Avery responded. Then his tone grew serious. "She's the most talented rider I've ever trained, Roberto. I think she could be great one day. She's got what it takes."

"*Si*," Roberto said, "yes, I can see that. You were right about her. Everything you said has proven to be true. And the colt, he too is just as I expected, a true son of Salome and Marius."

Avery said something else that Issie couldn't hear and then Roberto spoke once more.

"Does the girl know that you are her *bonifacio*?"

"No," Avery said. "Not yet. The time has never seemed right. And now that we are here, with the colt in this much danger…" He paused. "Roberto, what is your plan for getting Storm back?"

"There is no plan. We will simply run the race," Roberto said. "Marius is the best stallion in Spain and my son may be a headstrong boy, but he is our best rider. He will run the race and bring honour to El Caballo Danza Magnifico. That is how the colt will be returned to us."

Pressed back against the wall listening, Issie felt her breath catch in her throat. Avery was her *bonifacio*? What did that mean? And was that really Roberto's only plan to get Storm back? She wasn't going to sit back and wait for them to win the race. For all she knew, Vega could be putting the *serreta* on Storm right now! The race was not the answer. She knew now what she had to do. Vega was so arrogant, after the fiasco today the last thing he would ever expect would be for someone to fight back. Well, that arrogance would be his downfall. She was going to get her colt back the same way that he had been taken from her. She was going to steal him.

In her room, Issie quickly pulled on her jodhpurs and grabbed her *vaquero* hat before heading back down the stairs and out of the front door. The moment she was outside she was struck by just how hot the sun was. It was mid-afternoon, the time when the Andalusian sun reaches its peak and the *vaquero*s, weary from the heat, take a siesta. This afternoon nap would last for a couple of hours, until the sun sank lower and they could return once more to their work.

The heat and the siesta would work in her favour, Issie realised. There would be no need to talk her way round the men at Roberto's stables and convince them to let her take Angel out. The men were crashed out asleep on their cots in the bunkhouse. There would be no one at the stallions' stable block to stop her.

Angel was standing at the back of his stall in the shadows as always, but the stallion came forward without hesitation at the sound of Issie's voice.

"Hey, boy." Issie couldn't help feeling pleased that Angel was responding to her already. She reached out and ran her hand down the stallion's noble face, finding herself filled with pity all over again as she felt the ugly scar tissue that Vega had inflicted.

She thought of Storm now, in the hands of Vega. She

couldn't bear the thought of the *serreta* being used on him. Well, she thought, as she snatched the bridle off the hook in Angel's stall, she didn't need to worry about that for much longer. She would saddle up now and ride to Vega's hacienda. Vega's men would also be having their siesta when she arrived. She would be able to slip in and take her colt back in broad daylight, before anyone even realised she had been there. All she had to do was saddle up before anyone noticed her and—

"Going somewhere?"

A voice behind her made her jump. She spun round and saw a man standing there, wearing the traditional *vaquero* costume of El Caballo. In the darkness of the stable she thought at first that it was Roberto Nunez. Then the man stepped closer and she could see his face.

"Alfonso!" Issie said. "You scared me half to death! Don't sneak up on me like that."

"Taking Angel for a ride?" Alfonso said.

"Uh-huh…" Issie began to try and think of a fib she could tell him, something he would believe, but she could see by the look on Alfonso's face that he wouldn't be fooled.

"Let me guess," Alfonso said. "You're going after the colt. You're going to Vega's stables to bring him back, all by yourself?"

"No! Well, yes, but…" Issie tried to stay cool, but instead she found herself babbling. "Alfonso, I have to do it! He's got Storm. I need to get him back before Vega uses the *serreta* on him. I know you can't understand how much he means to me—"

"Hey! Hey!" Alfonso cut her off. "Calm down, you've got me all wrong. I'm not trying to stop you." He reached out and took the bridle off the hook outside Marius's stall and then turned to her and smiled. "I'm trying to tell you that I'm coming with you."

Chapter 10

Galloping together across the sunburnt fields of the El Caballo, the two great grey stallions, Marius and Angel, made an impressive sight. "Alfonso, you don't have to do this, you know," Issie shouted out. "Your dad will be furious when he finds out."

Alfonso was ahead of Issie, but now he pulled Marius up so that the two of them were riding together. "First of all, you must stop calling me Alfonso," he shouted back at her. "My friends all call me Alfie – OK?"

Issie nodded.

"And second," Alfie continued, "my dad is not as bad as you think. He's a pussycat once you get to know him. Right now it's all 'honour this' and 'tradition that'. He'd never agree to let us steal the colt – but you watch, when we bring Storm back home, he'll be totally on our side."

Issie had her doubts about this, but she wasn't going to argue. She hadn't argued with Alfie either when he'd insisted on coming with her. After all, as he pointed out, he knew his way into Vega's stables and she didn't. With him on her side, Issie stood a fighting chance of getting her colt back.

The two riders slowed down to a trot as they neared the gorge, and it was easier to talk as they rode side by side. "Your dad and Tom have known each other for a long time, huh?" Issie said.

"Yeah, twenty years. They met before I was even born," Alfie said. "Then Tom moved back to New Zealand, so I never really knew him. He and Dad used to write to each other. Dad would always be really happy when he got a letter from the other side of the world."

"It's kinda cool how close they are. They've been inseparable since we arrived," Issie said. "I guess they have a lot to catch up on."

Alfie nodded. "It's great to see my dad talking about old times again. He doesn't usually have anyone to talk to about that stuff. I think he gets lonely, you know? It's really isolated here and, I mean, he has me of course, and his *vaqueros*, but when Francoise and I are away with El Caballo

Danza Magnifico it must be very quiet at the hacienda."

"Where's your mum?" Issie asked. "Why doesn't she live with you?"

Alfie was quiet for a moment. "She died," he said, "when I was six."

"I'm sorry…" Issie felt dreadful. What a stupid thing to say! She hadn't realised.

"It's OK," Alfie said, "honest. It was a long time ago. I hardly remember her now. My dad brought me up by himself. And Francoise too, I suppose. Not like she's my stepmum or anything like that, but she joined El Caballo not long after that and she's always kept an eye on me, you know?"

Issie nodded. "My dad didn't die or anything, but he left when I was nine. I don't really see him. It's just me and Mum."

"You've got Tom," Alfie offered. "He seems to look out for you."

Issie felt a sting of guilt when Alfie said this. "Tom would be really upset if he knew what we were doing."

"In that case," Alfie said, kicking Marius on, "he had better not find out and we had better not get caught."

They had reached the gorge now and Alfie took the lead on Marius. "Follow me, I know the way," he called back over his shoulder. Issie stuck close behind him until they reached the end of the gorge and they pulled up side by side once more and halted their horses. This was the same spot Issie had halted with Francoise when she had first set eyes on Vega's hacienda. This time, though, they'd be riding across the wide plains that lay in front of them, and sneaking into Vega's own stables to take back her colt.

On the horizon, Vega's hacienda looked like an ancient Spanish prison. The walls that surrounded the estate were two metres high and made of crumbling bricks and plaster the colour of dried blood. The top of the wall had pointy turrets, like a Moorish castle, and over the top of the turrets Issie could make out the rooftops of Vega's hacienda.

"Vega's stables are at the back of the hacienda," Alfie said. He pointed at the orange grove to the right ahead of them. "We can tie the horses up there and then vault the wall into the garden. Once we find your colt, we'll have to take him back out of the main gates – it's the only way."

Issie nodded at this.

"Ready?" Alfie asked.

"Uh-huh," she replied.

"Then let's go!" And with that Alfie clucked his horse on and Issie followed, galloping across the green fields towards the hacienda.

As they got nearer to Vega's house, Issie could have sworn she felt Angel tense up underneath her, slowing his stride a little. She didn't urge him on. Instead, she spoke gently to the stallion, reassuring him with the softness of her voice. She had seen the way Angel had reacted when they met the mustachioed man that morning at the *feria* in the village square. Angel had been terrified of Vega and Issie sensed the same fear in her horse now. This hacienda, Vega's stables, had once been Angel's home – and it was not a home the stallion was keen to return to.

Is it any wonder? Issie thought. After all, the stallion still bore the marks of the *serreta* that Vega had forced on him, and the scars ran deep, beyond the marks on his face, all the way to the hidden recesses of Angel's mighty heart.

"It's OK," Issie reassured him, giving Angel a stroke along his proud, arched neck. "We're not staying there for long, I promise. We just need to find Storm and get straight out again."

They had reached the cover of the orange grove now, and the trees kept them hidden as they neared the high wall that ran around the hacienda. Alfie leapt down off

Marius's back and put a finger to his lips to signal that they needed to be quiet now. Then he led Marius towards an orange tree and tethered the horse by his reins. Issie did the same, whispering softly to Angel as she knotted the leather to the bough of the orange tree next to Marius.

"I'll be back soon," she told the stallion.

"Here!" Alfie hissed at her. "Give me a leg up on to the wall and then I'll pull you up."

Issie legged him up as if she was helping him on to a horse and then Alfie balanced on top of the wall, checking that the coast was clear before giving her his hand so she could climb up too. Issie perched there for a moment, hidden between the turrets, looking down at the gardens in the courtyard below. It was a grand Moorish garden filled with mosaic-tiled fountains, overgrown lantana and rows of tall palm trees. A maze created from neatly clipped conifers ran all the way from the house to the buildings at the rear of the hacienda, which Issie figured must be the stables.

"Follow me!" Alfie whispered. He jumped like a cat into the lantana bushes and Issie promptly followed him. The maze hedging kept them hidden from sight as they crept on, making their way towards the crumbling brick archways that led to the stables.

Issie had been right. It was siesta time and the whole

hacienda was cloaked in silence. There was no sound here except the gentle trickling of the garden fountains and the dry chirrup of the cicadas. She followed Alfie down the stairs and across the cobbles, through the archways that marked the entrance to the stable block.

Inside, the loose boxes ran in rows up either side of the long corridor. There must have been at least thirty loose boxes stretching ahead of them, and the doors to the boxes were solid wood, all shut tight and bolted. "He must be in one of these stalls," Alfie said. He began to unbolt the door to the first stall. "Let's start looking. I'll take the left side, you take the right."

"No," Issie said. "I know a faster way."

It was risky, whistling for her colt, but they didn't have time to search every stall. And so she pursed her lips together and blew.

Two short, sharp notes rang out in the stillness. Issie waited but no reply came. She took another breath, ready to try once more, but before she could whistle a second time, a shrill nicker returned her call.

"Storm!" she called out. There was another nicker and Issie focused, trying to follow the sound of the colt's cry. It was coming from the end of the stable block!

At the far end of the stables, Issie could see the light

flooding into the darkness through an archway that she decided must lead outside.

"He's down there!" She broke into a run and began heading towards the light with Alfie close behind her. Ahead of her, she could see that a wooden five-bar gate ran right across the width of the archway, blocking it off. Behind this gate was a small lawn enclosure, bordered by high stone walls. It was a sort of secret garden, with beds of mint and pomegranate trees and gnarled, ancient bougainvillea vines climbing the walls. It was also a prison as far as Issie was concerned because here, with his head craning over the wooden gate to meet her, was her colt. It was Storm!

As he saw the girl with the long dark hair running towards him the colt let out another nicker, more urgent this time, demanding her attention.

It's me, I'm right here! he seemed to be saying. He gave more soft little nickers of excitement, pacing back and forth behind the gate.

Issie, meanwhile, was running so hard she thought her heart would burst. She sprinted down the corridor to the gates, and when she finally reached the colt she was gasping to hold back her tears and to catch her breath.

"I know, I know," Issie said, choking with emotion as

she put her arms around the colt's neck and hugged him tight, "I missed you too. I was so worried! But don't worry, I'm here now and I'm going to…"

Their reunion was cut short. There was the sound of footsteps on the cobbles behind her. Issie turned round, expecting to see Alfie. What she didn't expect to see was that behind Alfie were three *vaquero*s, all running down the stable corridor heading towards them.

"We've got company!" Alfie said as he reached her side.

"Thanks for the warning," Issie said darkly. "Now how do we get Storm out of here?"

"No time for that now." Alfie shook his head. "We need to get out." He looked around frantically.

"There!" he said, pointing to the bougainvillea vine that was climbing up the wall of Storm's enclosure. "That's our way out. We can climb up that vine and out over the wall." He vaulted over the gate and ran past Storm. He gave the vines a tug. "They're strong enough to hold us, I think. Come on!" he said, already climbing up and getting a foothold on the top of the wall.

Issie hesitated. She didn't want to leave Storm's side so soon after finding him. But she had no choice. If these men caught her here, like this… Issie might have been brave, but she wasn't foolish. She had no desire to find out for herself what a man like Vega was capable of if he caught her trying to steal back her colt.

She followed Alfie over the gate and ran for the vines, shimmying up so that she could get a handhold on the top of the wall itself and pull herself over. She was relieved to see that the wall led back to the orange grove outside the estate where they had tethered the horses. Alfie was already mounted on Marius and waiting for her. She hit the ground running, sprinting towards Angel, who was fretting and pacing nervously, looking like he wanted to get away even more desperately than Issie did.

"Come on!" Alfie said impatiently. "They'll be getting their horses now, they'll come after us for sure."

Over the wall behind her, Issie could hear the shouts of the men. The *vaquero*s had disappeared and Issie guessed that they must have gone back to the stables to get their horses.

"C'mon, Angel," she said, struggling to unknot the leather reins from the orange tree. "We've gotta go."

Marius and Alfie had already galloped off and were almost clear of the orange grove, and Angel was keen to follow them. The stallion's keen ears could already hear the sound that Issie now heard. The thunder of hoofbeats in the air as the *vaquero*s mounted up and rode out of the hacienda gates, circling back through the orange grove, riding hard to hunt them down.

Issie mounted up and turned Angel round. Ahead of her, they had about thirty metres to ride through the orange grove before they hit the open pasture that would lead them back to the gorge and El Caballo. They needed to get clear of these *vaqueros* quickly if they were going to make it home to safety. She gathered up her reins and was about to kick Angel, but instead, she let out a scream. There was something holding her back!

She looked down in horror to see a face leering up at her. It was a *vaquero* and he had his fat hands wrapped tight around her ankle.

Issie screamed again and pulled hard, but the *vaquero* had grasped her boot with both hands and was hanging on tight. He yelled out to the other horsemen in Spanish to let them know that he had her, and then he looked up at Issie's terrified face.

"Let go of me!" she shrieked.

"What were you doing? Trying to take *Señor* Vega's colt, eh?" the man replied.

"He's not Vega's colt!" Issie said through gritted teeth. "He's mine!" Her anger gave her a new surge of energy and she wrenched her foot once more, pulling so hard that the boot came clean off in the man's meaty paws.

Issie took her chance, and before the *vaquero* could make another grab at her, Angel had lunged forward and broken into a gallop, leaving Vega's man standing there holding nothing more than an empty boot.

Issie slipped her sock foot back into the stirrup and rose up out of the saddle as Angel galloped on. They were almost clear of the orange trees and ahead of them was the grassy pasture that led to the entrance of the gorge that would take her back to El Caballo. Ahead of her, Alfie and Marius had almost a two-hundred-metre lead on them. The boy and the stallion weren't slowing down to wait for them either, they were galloping flat out.

Issie looked back over her shoulder. Sure enough, there were two more of Vega's *vaquero*s giving chase. Both of them were on powerful Lusitano stallions, and their horses were already in full gallop and gaining on Issie, their strides chewing up the distance between them.

"Angel!" Issie whispered, rising even higher in her stirrups so that she was resting on her knees with her body low over the grey stallion's neck. "Angel, come on, boy. We need to stay ahead of them. Let's go! *Vamos!*"

The grey horse was already galloping, but as Issie asked more of him, he seemed to sense the danger and respond to the urgency of her plea. His stride suddenly lengthened and his frame extended so that the ground was swallowed up by his gallop. Issie bent down even lower and wrapped her hands in the stallion's mane, gripping tightly in case the horse swerved and she lost her seat. She needn't have worried. Angel was running as straight as an arrow towards the gorge, following behind Marius and galloping as if his life depended on it. His neck was flecked with foam and his flanks were heaving as he kept lengthening his stride, his pace increasing all the time as he drew further and further away from the horsemen behind him and closer and closer to the horse in front of him.

Issie could see now why Francoise had said that she chose Angel because of his speed. Although the stallion had the powerful muscles of an Andalusian, his gallop was more like that of a thoroughbred. He ran with a lightness and a grace that belied his burly physique. He had stamina too, maintaining his speed as Marius began to tire and drop back.

Marius had been way ahead of Angel, but now the distance between the two stallions had closed up so that the two horses were only a length apart. Angel was gaining more and more with every stride. Issie bent down even lower over the stallion's withers and kept talking to him, urging him on. Then Angel pulled up alongside Marius so that the two stallions were neck and neck and Issie and Alfie were next to each other.

As the two horses galloped towards the gorge Angel was powering forward with every stride, getting ahead of Marius and opening up his lead on the other stallion. For a moment, as Angel surged past the dapple-grey, Issie looked over and saw Alfie frantically urging his horse on, trying to coax the speed out of Marius to keep up with Angel. But it was useless.

As they reached the gorge Angel was in the lead, ahead of Marius by nearly two lengths, and the stallion still had plenty of running in him.

Issie cast a glance back over her shoulder. Angel had outrun Vega's men too. They had given up and pulled their horses back to a trot. They were far in the distance, no longer a threat.

It was then that Issie realised what had just happened. They had come here to get her colt and they had failed, but in the process she had discovered something almost as important. Angel was faster than Marius. The two horses had just been pitted against each other in the race of their lives – and Angel had won.

Chapter 11

Even though they had left the *vaquero*s in their dust back at the entrance to the gorge, Issie still didn't stop checking over her shoulder until they reached the gates of El Caballo.

"Are you OK?" Alfie asked her as he slid down off Marius's back and threw the reins over the horse's neck to lead him back to the stables.

"Uh-huh," Issie said. She vaulted down from Angel's back and as she hit the ground she felt the cobblestones beneath her sock foot and realised she only had one boot on. She had come so close to being caught! During the chase everything had happened so fast she hadn't had time to be scared, but now it was over, she realised that she was shaking uncontrollably.

Going to Vega's hacienda had been a stupid, desperate thing to do, she could see that now. The others were right – this wasn't the way to get her colt back. She and Alfie had been lucky to get away – in fact she never would have escaped if it weren't for Angel. She had never ridden a horse capable of such speed. Angel hadn't just outrun Vega's horses – he had raced them into the ground. Not only that, he had beaten Marius. There had been at least two hundred metres separating the stallion from Marius and yet he had caught him up as if Marius was standing still.

Angel's neck was wet with foamy sweat and his flanks were heaving from the run, yet his nerves were still wired up from his gallop and he didn't seem at all tired. Francoise had clearly been working on his fitness during her rides around El Caballo. The stallion was race-fit, and the gallop from Vega's hadn't exhausted him. In fact, it only served to excite him. As Issie tried to cool him down and bring him back to a walk, Angel kept skipping and dancing, refusing to settle as Issie led him back towards the stables. She spoke to the stallion in a soft, low voice, her tone calming him, as she stroked his broad, glistening white crest.

"He's fast, huh?" Alfie said as he led Marius up to walk back to the stables alongside her.

"Yeah," Issie agreed. "Francoise said he'd been bred for speed. I guess she was right."

Alfie nodded. He didn't look particularly happy. Finally he spoke again.

"He's faster than Marius," he said darkly. "He beat us, back there. I was riding as fast as I could when we left Vega's and you were way behind me, but you caught us easily."

Issie knew what Alfie was thinking. She was about to say something, but before she had the chance there was a shout from the stable block and Francoise and Avery came running towards them.

When Francoise saw the state the horses were in she knew immediately what they had done.

"Tell me you didn't!" she said, aghast, as she snatched Marius's reins from Alfie. "Tell me you didn't go to Vega's!"

"We did," Issie said, "and we saw Storm."

"We nearly had him too," Alfie added, "but Vega's men woke up and they chased us. We only just got away."

The look of concern on Francoise's face turned to anger. "I cannot believe this!" She shook her head in disbelief. "How could you both defy us like this? Alfie, your father told you that it was too risky to face Vega!"

"We weren't going to face him," Issie said. "We were going to bring Storm back."

"Don't play clever, Isadora," Avery said. "You know that Francoise is right. Vega is a dangerous man. I can't believe you two would be so foolish."

Issie was about to answer back, but when she looked at her instructor's face she saw something there that stopped her. She had never seen Avery so angry – and she realised at that moment just how deeply worried he must have been when he'd found that both Issie and Angel were missing.

"I'm really sorry, Tom." Issie bit her bottom lip. "I know it was a dumb thing to do, but I just wanted to get Storm back so badly."

Francoise shook her head, furious. "It is a miracle that you both escaped. I do not want to think about what might have happened if they had caught you."

"They nearly did catch Issie, but she got away!" Alfie said.

Issie shot Alfie a look, wishing that he would shut up. She didn't want Tom to know just how close she had come to being caught by Vega's men.

"I was at least twenty lengths ahead of her on Marius, and she caught me up," Alfie continued. "Angel totally outran Marius, I've never seen a horse go that fast. We were galloping flat out and he came up behind us like a rocket."

"Alfie's right. You should have seen him run," Issie

said. "Those *vaquero*s were right behind him one moment and then I asked him to run harder and he did it. He stretched out and there was no way they were going to catch him. He caught up to Marius and he passed him before we'd hit the gorge. He's fast all right, Francoise, just like you said he was."

Issie looked at Francoise, her heart racing. "Francoise, how far do you think it is from Vega's hacienda to the gorge?"

Francoise's eyes narrowed. She had already guessed what Issie was thinking. "It is about two kilometres, maybe a little more," she said.

"What are you talking about?" Avery was confused. But the other two knew exactly what Issie was driving at.

"She means the race," Alfie said. "The Silver Bridle."

Issie nodded. "Angel totally outran Vega's horses today. And he was faster than Marius. What if he could do the same in the race?" Issie held her breath for a moment and then she blurted out the words. "I think we should race Angel in the Silver Bridle. I think he can win."

"Isadora," Francoise said, "El Caballo Danza Magnifico already has a champion. Marius will be racing for us in the Silver Bridle. It has been decided."

"But why?" Issie said. "Francoise, you said yourself that Angel has the bloodlines of great racehorses in him. If he's faster than Marius, then shouldn't we race him instead?"

Francoise shook her head. "Angel has not been in training as Marius has…"

"…and yet he still managed to beat Vega's horses by at least twenty lengths!" Issie insisted. "You said you'd been riding him, Francoise, galloping him over the hills. Well, it's worked. He's fit and he's ready to race. Besides, we have a whole week yet before the race. We could train him."

"*Oui*," Francoise conceded, "yes, potentially it could be done. What you say is true. Angel is strong and sound but…" she shook her head, "… this is madness. It is not possible for him to race. Alfie is our rider. He is the best in our stables, and you know he cannot ride Angel."

Avery was confused by this. "Why not?"

"Because Angel is scared of men," Alfie responded immediately. And at that moment Issie realised why Alfie looked so distraught when they had been walking the horses back to the stables. Alfie was supposed to ride El Caballo's champion in the Silver Bridle. But what if Angel were really faster than Marius?

"I can't ride Angel," Alfie continued. "Believe me, I've tried. He's thrown me every time I got on his back. Vega using the *serreta* terrified him. It made him afraid, not just of Vega but all men – including me."

"It is not uncommon, this fear of men," Francoise said. "I have known many horses to object to having male riders. But in Angel's case? It is much more than mere objection. His fear of men is absolute. Angel cannot be ridden by a man."

"Francoise?" Issie said. "Francoise, what if it wasn't a man? What if it wasn't Alfie riding him? What if it was a woman?"

"That is impossible," Francoise said. "In case you haven't noticed, my arm is broken – and the race is just a week away. And anyway—"

"I didn't mean you!" Issie said. "I meant me. I can ride him."

The Frenchwoman shook her head. "No, no! Let me finish. It is not possible for you or any woman to ride. In the history of the Silver Bridle, the riders for each hacienda have always, always been men. Women do not race."

Issie furrowed her brow. "So are you saying it's against the rules for a girl to ride?"

Alfie shook his head. "It's not the rules, exactly. It's tradition. But traditions are strong here. You know what my dad is like."

"But your dad would understand. If Angel is the fastest horse then he'd want Angel to run, wouldn't he? If it's not actually against the rules? I mean, *if* I could convince Roberto, if I could get him to let me ride Angel, then they wouldn't be able to stop me?"

"No," Francoise admitted. "They wouldn't be able to stop you."

"Then we should ask Roberto to let me ride," Issie said.

"Now hold on a minute," Avery said. "Issie, I think you need to get a grip. Roberto will never allow this. The Silver Bridle is not just any horse race, it's a duel on horseback, a contest where horses and men routinely risk their lives to win."

"Tom is right," Francoise agreed. "The men who ride this race are battle-hardened. Once they are in that village square and the bell rings to signal the start, they will fight like animals to win."

"If I could get a good start and ride Angel like I did today then it wouldn't matter," Issie insisted. "We'd be out in front the whole way and no one would even have the chance to touch us."

"This is crazy even to talk about this," Francoise sighed. "Even if we were all in agreement, what then? You would still have to convince Roberto." She paused. "This race is of the utmost importance to him. He has focused all his energy on training Marius for this day.

It will be impossible for him to change his mind now."

"It's true," Alfie said. "You've seen my father in action, Issie. He's not a man who is easily persuaded."

Issie knew this was true. She found the idea of facing up to Roberto scarier than any horse race. Since they had arrived at El Caballo, Roberto had been the perfect host, kind and generous. But there was also something that made Issie nervous around him. Roberto had kept a cool distance from her ever since she arrived. And his conversation in the living room with Avery made it clear that he thought she was... what was the word he used? Impetuous!

To Roberto, Issie was nothing more than a troublesome kid. Convincing him that she was capable of riding in the race was not going to be easy.

"Francoise?" Issie said hopefully. "Will you ask him? Will you tell Roberto that Angel should race?"

Francoise shook her head. "No, Isadora. It would do no good. Roberto thinks you are just a child. If you want him to let you ride, then it is up to you to convince him that you can take on the *vaquero*s and beat them at their own game."

"Francoise is right," Alfie agreed. "My father is a man of honour. You stand a better chance of winning his respect if you ask him yourself."

"If you want to race Angel, it is up to you," Francoise said. "Isadora, you alone are the one. You must talk to Roberto Nunez."

Chapter 12

The indoor training school at El Caballo Danza Magnifico was a spectacular space. With its vaulted ceilings and horse tapestries hanging at the entranceways, it had the feel of a grand cathedral – one with an Olympic-sized dressage arena in the middle of it.

This training arena was the very heart of El Caballo Danza Magnifico. All the schooling for the *haute école* horses took place here. The spectacular shows that the Spanish stallions performed around the world required years of training and it all happened right here.

At this very moment the famed El Caballo stallions were in the middle of a training session, rehearsing their latest routine for the upcoming world tour. As Issie entered the school in search of Roberto her eyes fell upon the stallions and the vision took her breath away.

In the arena, twelve perfect, white horses were marching in unison, lifting their legs up in a high, exaggerated Spanish Walk. One by one the stallions wheeled about, pirouetting, striking off at precisely the same time to dance a half-pass back across the sand.

It was a performance that any horse-lover in the world would have paid handsomely to see, and here was Issie, all alone, with a front row seat, watching the greatest performing horses in the business at work.

She gazed on, enraptured, as the elegant stallions, their manes cascading down their necks like white silk, tails flowing behind them like bridal trains, began to circle the arena, showing off their extended trot – their legs flicking out in front of them like ballerinas *en pointe*, graceful and poised…

"Stop! Stop!" There was a voice over the sound system. The riders, immediately aware that something was not right, pulled their horses up to a halt and turned their heads to look up at the man above them, sitting enclosed in a glass booth that looked down over the arena. Issie looked up there too and saw Roberto, sitting behind the microphone in the booth.

Roberto spoke again into the microphone and his voice

echoed out through the speakers in the arena. "Very good pirouettes," he said, "lovely collection! But then what happened when you were doing the extended trot? I expect these horses to look like they are floating above the sand, not just trotting along like it's a hack in the park! Remember when you ask for the trot to really drive them forward with your hips to get their legs active."

He muttered something in Spanish that Issie didn't understand and then spoke again clearly into the microphone. "We're going to take it from the very start again. This time, I want to see their hooves strike the ground exactly on the beat of the castanets. OK? Let's take it from the top!"

Roberto was about to say something else when he spotted Issie at the side of the arena. He gave her a wave. "Isadora, you are welcome to come up and join me in here," he spoke into the microphone. "Use the steps at the back of the arena – the hallway leads you up to the booth."

Issie did as he said, walking between the rows of tiered seating towards the far corner of the arena until she found the stairwell that led up to the glass viewing booth where Roberto was sitting.

Roberto greeted her warmly with a kiss on both cheeks. "You came to watch the horses train?"

Issie didn't know what to say. She was too nervous to bring up the real reason for her visit. "Why did you stop them just now?" she asked. "I was watching them do the extended trot and I thought they looked OK. What was wrong with it?"

Roberto shook his head. "It was no good. Not enough elevation, not enough… magic. El Caballo Danza Magnifico has the best horses in the world – watching them perform must be more than just *OK*." He stressed the word as if he found it distasteful. "They must be magnificent. It is easy to produce horses that can perform a reasonable pirouette or half-pass, but here we are always striving to reach the utmost levels of the *haute école*. It is that final polish that will make the crowd gasp with delight or cry with pure joy. This is what we must aim for."

Roberto beckoned for Issie to take a seat next to him. Then he slid down the yellow button on the control desk in front of him and the lights in the arena faded to black. He pressed another button on the console and the music began once more, the sound of the Spanish flamenco. As the castanets began to strike up, Roberto slid the lights back on, the signal for the horses to enter the ring to start the routine again. Issie watched as they came in single file down the centre line of the arena, peeling off one by one in each direction.

"I've seen this before," she said to Roberto, "in Chevalier Point, when El Caballo was on tour. I saw them perform this routine."

"We have changed it a little since then," Roberto said. "There is a whole new dance for the Anglo-Arab mares to perform also."

He took his eyes off the Lipizzaners in front of him now and turned to look at Isadora.

"Tell me," he said, "how is Salome? The mare that you call Blaze. Is she happy in your country? She must miss her old life, running with the herd under the heat of the Spanish sun. She is so far from home, it must be very strange for her."

Issie had never thought about it like that before. As far as she was concerned, Blaze was home. OK, so the mare had grown up here at El Caballo, but she was Issie's horse now, and she knew Blaze loved her life in Chevalier Point.

"She's great," Issie said. "I haven't ridden her since Storm was born, and it's winter at home, but when the weather gets better I'll be able to ride her again."

Roberto smiled. "She is not an easy mare to ride. Anglo-Arabs can be highly strung and Salome is no exception. It is impressive that you can handle her. Avery tells me that you are a very good rider."

Issie squirmed nervously. This seemed like a good time to ask Roberto the question that she had come here with. "Roberto, I wanted to talk to you... It's about the Silver Bridle."

"What about it?" Roberto stiffened in his seat. He could see that Issie had something important on her mind.

"I know that you think that Marius can win the race," Issie began, "but what if there was an even faster horse in your stable?"

Roberto shook his head. "Impossible. I am quite certain. Marius is my best stallion. Alfonso has raced him against every horse in my stable to prove it!"

"Not every horse," Issie said.

Roberto looked at her. "And which horse is it that you suggest? Who do you think is faster than Marius?"

"Angel," Issie said. "I think Angel should be your champion to race in the Silver Bridle."

Roberto shook his head. "Did Francoise not explain to you?" he asked. "Angel is afraid of men. All of the men in my stable have attempted to ride him. He will not have a man on his back – not even Alfonso, and he is my best rider."

"Angel's scared of men – but he's not scared of women," Issie said. "He's not scared of me. I can ride him, Roberto!"

"You?" Roberto looked hard at her. "How old are you? Fourteen? You are not a grown woman. You are not much more than a child."

"I'm old enough. I rode him today – he was faster than Marius. You can ask Francoise and Alfie – they'll back me up."

Roberto raised an eyebrow. "You raced against Marius?"

"I didn't mean to race him – it just kind of happened. Alfie and I were riding back across the high pasture and Angel totally beat him to the other side. Marius had a twenty-length lead on us and we overtook him."

Roberto's eyes narrowed. "The high pasture? You were near Vega's hacienda?"

Issie winced at this. She had been hoping Roberto wouldn't question how she came to be racing against Marius.

"Umm… yeah, Alfie was showing me around. You know, a full tour of the estate," she offered. It was a feeble excuse, but Roberto seemed to let it slide.

"Anyway, it makes no difference if Angel beat Marius racing on the high pasture," Roberto continued. "The Silver Bridle is not raced on open fields. This is no ordinary race, it is a street fight, a rough contest, ridden by men who will stop at nothing to win. It is no place for a girl."

"But Angel can win. I know he can!" Issie said. "Please, Roberto, let me prove it to you. Let Angel race Marius again. We can race on the streets of the square this time and that will prove to you that I can handle it. Then you'll have to let Angel take Marius's place in the race."

Roberto bristled at this. "Have to? I do not have to do anything, Isadora. I understand that this race means a lot to you also – your colt is at stake. Still, it is up to me to decide who races for El Caballo. It is not your choice to make."

Issie opened her mouth to speak, but Roberto raised a hand. "Wait!" he said. "I did not say no, did I? If Angel is as fast as you say he is, then I want to see it for myself. We shall have a match race as you suggest. Tomorrow we shall take both the horses to the village square and see whether you are right. If your horse can run as fast as he did in the fields, then he will be our champion for the Silver Bridle. But if he does not win, then you must accept it, and stand back and let Alfie and Marius take up the flag for El Caballo instead. Does that sound fair?"

Issie was overcome with excitement. "Thank you, Roberto. Thank you for giving me this chance!"

"You have much courage for one so young." Roberto

smiled at her. "You will need all of it to best my son in this match race."

"I won't let you down," Issie said. "You'll see. Angel will prove how fast he is tomorrow."

Roberto raised an eyebrow at this, then he said, "Tell me, Isadora, what will happen if we do win the Silver Bridle?"

"What do you mean?" Issie was confused.

"You will get your colt back," Roberto said. "And what then? What will you do with him? Take him home to your pony club at Chevalier Point?"

"Why?" Issie said. "Is there something wrong with that? He's my horse!" She could feel her pulse racing now. What did Roberto mean? Was he planning to try and take the colt off her?

"Do not panic," Roberto said gently. "You must know by now, the colt is yours and no one at El Caballo would dream of taking him away from you."

"Then why wouldn't I take him home with me?"

"Because he is already home," Roberto said. "Isadora, look around you here. You are standing in one of the greatest horse training institutions in the whole world. This is where Nightstorm is meant to be. Leave him here with us and we will train him for you. He can receive schooling here with the best riders in the world. He'll be taught *haute école* movements, far above anything that he might learn at pony club. We could fulfil the destiny of his bloodlines, make him a true El Caballo stallion."

"Why would you do that? What would be in it for you?"

"You know how important Nightstorm's bloodlines are to us," Roberto said. "When Nightstorm comes of age, we would use him as a sire across our best mares. His progeny, his colts and fillies, would be invaluable for El Caballo. Then, with Nightstorm's training completed, and with our fields full of his foals, we could return him to you."

Issie didn't know what to say.

"Do not answer me now," Roberto told her. "Please, take your time and think about it. Search your heart. For you must know that this farm is Nightstorm's true home. Just as it is still the home of his mother, Salome."

"Her name isn't Salome – it's Blaze," Issie said, "and her home is with me in Chevalier Point, just like Storm."

Roberto was quiet for a moment. When he finally spoke, his voice was soft and low. "I can see the great love that you have for your horses, Isadora," he said. "It burns like a fire in you," and then he added, "but love does not always mean keeping things close to your heart. Sometimes it can also mean letting them go."

He looked down at the arena where the stallions were now finishing their routine. The Lipizzaners were taking their bows, each horse lowering itself down on to one knee to bow its head, while the riders on their backs doffed their hats to the imaginary audience.

"They have finished. I must go down to the arena now to discuss their training. They have much that they need to improve on," Roberto told her. "I am sorry our conversation must end here. But we will talk again, I am sure. With the race coming, there is much to be decided."

"Yes," Issie agreed. "There really is."

At dinner that night, Issie was surprised when Roberto poured her a glass of *fino* sherry, just like the adults had, and then raised his glass.

"I would like to propose a toast," Roberto said. "We are lucky to have friends here with us from across the world, friends who love and value their horses as much as we do. Tomorrow my son Alfie and Isadora will have their match race to see which of them will ride for the Silver Bridle and the glory of El Caballo Danza Magnifico. I wish them both luck. *Viva El Caballo!*"

"*Viva El Caballo!*" everyone cried, raising their glasses.

Avery, though, did not raise his glass. It was clear he was not happy with Roberto's decision, but he said nothing.

Issie, who was sitting next to Alfie, took a sip of her sherry. It was dry and almost bitter. "It doesn't taste anything like the stuff that Granny has in her sideboard at home," she said to Alfie.

"That depends on who your grandma is," Alfie smiled. He began to eat his paella.

"Umm, Alfie?" Issie said. "I know that the Silver Bridle is, like, a really big thing for you. I just want to say that I'm not trying to take your place. If there was any way that you could ride Angel instead of me…"

Alfie smiled at her. "Yes, the race is a big deal for me. I have been training for it my whole life. Ever since I was a young boy I knew I wanted to ride in the Silver Bridle and bring honour to El Caballo."

"I'm really sorry—" Issie began, but he cut her off.

"My ego will be bruised if you beat me, Issie, but the most important thing is for El Caballo to win against Vega, so that we can get your colt back and our horses too. If you and Angel are faster than me and Marius, then I will accept that."

"Thank you." Issie smiled.

"Hey!" Alfie said. "Don't thank me yet – you still haven't won. Don't get me wrong, I plan to beat you tomorrow, Isadora. Once we are lined up on that race course we will no longer be friends, we will be adversaries. My dad has given me instructions to treat you like any other rival for the Silver Bridle. Kicking, pushing, even biting the other riders, nothing is outlawed in this race. You must be prepared for anything."

"You're kidding me, right?" Issie couldn't believe it.

"We will see tomorrow, won't we?" Alfie replied.

Avery, who had been listening to their conversation, didn't say anything, but after dinner as they were all heading for their rooms he pulled Issie aside.

"I heard what Alfie was saying to you at dinner," Avery said. "Issie, I cannot believe you're going through with this. I never thought for a moment that Roberto would agree to it, or I would have put my foot down earlier." Avery looked serious. "This match race could get rough. I think you need to reconsider."

Issie shook her head. "I can handle it, Tom. I'm not scared."

"That's the problem. You should be," Avery replied. "Issie, I don't want to risk you getting hurt—"

"Please, Tom," Issie said. "Don't try and talk me out

of it. I've been feeling so helpless ever since we got here and everyone keeps treating me like I'm just this little girl. Now I've managed to convince Roberto to let me race, and if you force me to back out again then he'll think I'm just a silly kid."

Avery shook his head. "I'm not happy about this. I wish you'd reconsider. At least promise me you'll play it safe?"

Issie smiled. "You've got my word on it."

The match race was planned for early the next morning. Issie had woken up with her tummy in a tight ball of nerves and so she decided to skip breakfast. She pulled on her jodhpurs and boots and headed down to the stables. When she arrived, she found Alfie, Roberto and Avery already there waiting for her.

"Francoise has saddled up Angel for you. She's just getting Marius ready now," Avery told Issie. "We'll all be riding together up to the village."

Alfie smiled at Issie as he adjusted his helmet. "Did you sleep well?" he asked. "Are you ready to race?"

Issie was about to reply when she was interrupted by shouts coming from the stables. The grooms in the stallions' quarters were yelling about something. Issie couldn't make out what they were saying. She could hear Francoise's voice over all the others' though, and she sounded really upset. She was speaking in Spanish so Issie didn't have a clue what she was on about, but Roberto clearly understood her. His face fell as he heard Francoise's cries and then he was running for the stables with Alfie right behind him.

Avery and Issie instinctively followed after them, running across the cobbled courtyard. They had almost reached the stallions' quarters when Francoise emerged in front of them. She was leading Marius and immediately Issie could see that something was very wrong with the grey stallion. Francoise was trying to make Marius walk forward, but the horse was refusing to move properly. As Issie and the others looked on in horror, Francoise coaxed him to take a few more tentative steps, and it became clear that Marius was favouring his near front leg. The stallion was placing his hoof gingerly on the ground, as if he were afraid to put his weight on it. He made one more noble effort and tried to hobble forward for another stride or so, then he gave up and lifted the leg up, holding it aloft pitifully in midair. Issie saw Francoise shaking her head, and the look of complete despair on Roberto's face as the reality of the disaster they were witnessing sank in.

There would be no match race today. Marius, the great hope for the Silver Bridle, the finest stallion of El Caballo Danza Magnifico, was lame.

Chapter 13

It was a tense wait back at El Caballo Danza Magnifico while the vet examined Marius. When he finally emerged from the stallion's loose box, shaking his head as he spoke to Roberto, they all knew the news wasn't good.

"It's a ripped tendon," the vet confirmed as they gathered around. "My guess is that it was caused by the stress of galloping on hard, uneven ground. Has this horse been ridden fast across country recently?"

Alfie and Issie both looked guiltily at each other, thinking about their escape from Vega's hacienda.

"How bad is it?" Alfie asked nervously. He was as white as a sheet as he asked the question they all wanted the answer to. "Will he still be able to race?"

The vet nodded solemnly. "He'll heal all right – but

not in time to race on Saturday. An injury like this needs time, the leg has to mend. It'll be at least a month before he can be ridden again."

"Thank you, Hector," Roberto said quietly. "I appreciate your help, coming here so quickly to examine him."

"I'm very sorry it couldn't be better news, Roberto," the vet said. "I know how much this horse means to El Caballo Danza Magnifico. If it is any consolation, you should know that the injury could have happened at any time. Perhaps it is better for it to have happened now than for the horse to break down halfway through the race."

Roberto didn't say anything. He walked on with the vet towards the wrought-iron gates of the hacienda and the vet continued to talk as he got into his car, telling Roberto about the medication he had prescribed for Marius, and advising him on strapping the leg until the tendons began to heal.

As he drove off, Roberto walked back across the cobbled courtyard to join the others who had been standing watching in silence.

"Dad," Alfie began, "it's all my fault. I should never have taken him out and galloped him this close to the race. It was—"

Roberto raised his hand to stop him. "Alfonso, you

heard the vet. There was a weakness in his tendon and this could have happened at any time. If he had not hurt his leg in this way, then perhaps he might have broken down in the Silver Bridle and been beaten."

Roberto turned to Issie. "Isadora, you shall get your wish. You wanted to ride Angel in the Silver Bridle? You will get to do exactly that."

"You mean—" Issie started to say.

"Without Marius, I have to race another horse," Roberto said. "Angel is the fastest stallion in my possession. And I have no choice in the matter but to put you on his back. So it is decided. You will line up at the starting rope as our champion on Saturday. The fate of El Caballo Danza Magnifico, and of your colt, is now in your hands."

Back at the villa, Issie still couldn't believe what had just happened.

"Roberto must hate me," she said to Avery.

"Why on earth would you think that?" he said.

"Because this is all my fault. I was the one who decided to go to Vega's to get Storm back. If Alfie hadn't come with me then Marius would never have got injured…"

"… or he might have broken down during the race itself and it could have been much worse," Avery finished her sentence. "Issie, you heard what the vet said. That stallion's tendon could have ripped at any time. I know that Roberto doesn't blame you."

"He'll blame me if I lose the race on Saturday, though, won't he?"

Avery looked worried. "Issie, this is too much pressure for Roberto or anyone to put on you, making you responsible for the future of El Caballo. Listen, Roberto is my friend. I'll talk to him, tell him that I will race instead. I can ride Sorcerer – he's fast enough."

"No, Tom!" Issie said. "Angel is the fastest horse and you know it."

"Issie," Avery said, "I'm your guardian here and I'm putting my foot down. I'm going to ride in your place."

"Tom, you can't. I have to do this. Sorcerer isn't ready. You'll lose and then Roberto will lose his five best horses to Vega. He's already got Storm and he's bound to choose Marius – maybe Angel too!"

"Maybe," Avery said, "but I'd rather lose the horses than risk your life."

"There are always risks! What about riding at Badminton?" Issie shot back. "I bet that was a risk when you did it the first time. And how about when you rode at the Olympics? Did you know the risks then, Tom? Riders make their own choices. Now I'm making mine. I know it's hard, but you have to let me grow up. Let me do this. Angel can win this race, but he can't do it without me – please, let me ride."

"There are other ways, Issie," Avery said. "I don't want you to get hurt. It's too dangerous. You heard what Alfie said about the other riders. They'll fight you and you're too small to fight them back."

"No, they won't." Issie shook her head. "They won't fight me. Not if I get away fast enough at the break. Tom, what if I could get Angel out in the lead right from the start and stay there the whole way? If we were out in front and Angel could hold the lead ahead of the other riders then they'd never get the chance to push me around."

Avery considered this for a moment. "It could work, I suppose," he said, "but you'd have to be lightning-quick at the break to make sure you got out in front straight away."

"I've already thought about that," Issie said. "Angel has the speed to do it, he just needs the training, so that he'd be certain to take off from the start line before all the other horses."

"So you're going to teach him to break?" Avery said.

"No," Issie replied hopefully, "you are." She looked at Avery. "Please, Tom, I can't do this without your help. I need you to be my trainer."

The next day was Tuesday – which meant that Avery and Issie had just four days to train Angel before they faced Vega in the village square.

Avery had told Issie to meet him at the stables bright and early on Tuesday morning, and when she got there she found her instructor in the tack room.

"I've been making some modifications to Angel's saddle," he said. The traditional *vaquero* stirrups, cast from black iron and clunky as a suit of armour, had been removed. Avery had replaced them with lightweight stainless-steel stirrups. "I found these in an old box stacked under the saddle blankets – they're just what you need," Avery said. "Those other stirrups are fine for *vaquero*s who ride with their legs hanging long, but for racing you need smaller stirrups so that you can balance up high in the saddle."

Avery took the saddle out into the courtyard, and Issie followed behind him.

"Umm, Tom?" she said. "Where are you going? Angel is in the other direction."

"I know," Avery said, "but in case you've forgotten, Angel is not very fond of men and I happen to be one. Once you get on his back it will be almost impossible for me to handle him. So if you want me to teach you how to ride a racehorse we're going to have to do it before you get on his back."

"How?" Issie didn't understand.

Avery took the saddle now and slung it over a hay bale in the corner of the courtyard.

"Climb up on that," he said.

"You want me to ride a hay bale?" Issie frowned.

"Why not? Are you worried it's going to buck you off?" Avery grinned. Then he explained. "The idea is to get your position right in the saddle before you mount up on Angel. Racehorse jockeys have a different centre of gravity. They ride with very short stirrups. Hop up on the saddle here and I'll show you."

"OK, but I feel pretty silly," Issie grumbled as she clambered up and threw herself into the saddle. She let her feet dangle down because the stirrups seemed to be adjusted so that the leathers were really short.

"Put your feet in the irons and tell me how they feel," Avery instructed her.

"I feel like a bird on a perch!" Issie giggled. "Look how high my knees are! It feels weird."

Avery eyed her up carefully, and shook his head. "They're the perfect length, you just need to get used to them – you're riding like a jockey now."

"Well, I don't know how they do it," Issie said.

Avery climbed up next to her on the hay bales, crouching down as if he were the jockey on his horse. "You need to tilt forward like me. It's a bit like two-point jumping position. You keep your weight over his wither and stay low. Your aim is to stay off his back and let him run. It will make you twice as fast around the track."

"I don't get it," Issie said. "My legs are up so high, how do I make him go?"

"Urge him on with your arms," Avery replied, "and give him little taps with your ankles and increase these as you want to go faster. It's easy, really."

Issie looked at him quizzically. "How do you know all this?"

"I rode trackwork for a few years," Avery said. "I had big plans to be a jockey."

"Why didn't you?"

"I grew two feet too tall!" Avery grinned.

"So you never raced?"

Avery shook his head. "Afraid not, but I rode the training sessions like a demon. I even had a nickname.

They used to call me 'The Spaceman' because I had a knack of finding the smallest space on the inside rail and slipping through it. I'd sit back and wait at the back of the field until we were right down to the wire and then I'd kick on and make my move. Always go for the inside rail, Issie, that's the fastest way. No matter how small the space may look, if you're a smart rider you can make it."

Avery paused. "Not that you'll be riding with tactics like that. You need to get out in front of the other riders right from the start. It'll surprise them when you take an early lead. They won't be expecting it. Once you're out in front, Angel must hold that lead. He's got the stamina to maintain the gallop the whole two kilometres, for three laps of the track. If you ride the race like I show you, they'll be left in your dust." Avery smiled. "Anyway, are you ready to get off the hay bales and start training a real horse?"

Issie felt the butterflies surging in her tummy. "I guess so."

"Then let's go saddle up."

With Avery riding by her side on Sorcerer, Issie headed out of the gates of El Caballo. She was practising her new jockey position, standing up in her short stirrups, keeping her weight centred over Angel's wither, but she nearly lost her balance when Avery turned Sorcerer to the left and headed up the dirt road in the opposite direction from the village.

Issie was confused. "Aren't we going to the village to train in the square?"

Avery shook his head. "I talked to Roberto about it last night. We both decided that training Angel in the village is too risky. It's full of gossips and Vega probably already knows that Marius is lame and Angel is racing in his place. We don't need Vega's spies watching us while we train and telling him what we're up to."

"So where are we going?" Issie asked.

"Follow me, you'll see," Avery said.

The two riders cantered up and around the winding roads that led to the peak of the olive hills behind El Caballo and a few minutes later they had reached the rise of a hill overlooking flat fields. The fields directly below them were planted with olives, but beyond the olive trees was a flat, barren plain, perfect for riding trackwork.

"This is where we'll train him," Avery said. "Do you see those trees over there? They mark the edge of the course. Then you take him all the way to the old stone building there, and then back to me. That's about two kilometres – the same distance as the Silver Bridle."

Avery pulled a stopwatch out of his pocket.

"What's that for?" Issie asked.

"Timing you," Avery said. "On a decent track, a fast racehorse can do two kilometres in a little under two minutes thirty. I want to get a sense of how fast Angel is."

Avery scratched a line in the dirt with his shoe right next to a tall olive tree.

"This is your start line. Now I don't want you to take him flat out, the first time around just breeze him, OK?"

Issie looked puzzled.

"It's a racing term," Avery said. "It means ride him at a medium pace. Let him gallop, but don't push him."

Issie did up the strap on her helmet.

"Take it easy this time. We'll see how he goes," Avery said and Issie lined the stallion up.

"On your marks, get set… go!"

Avery dropped his hand and Issie took the cue, letting go of her tight grip on the reins. Angel lunged forward, breaking like a racehorse. His burst of speed was so sudden that for a moment Issie was left behind the stallion's movement and had to snatch at his mane to hang on. She looked down and saw the ground rushing beneath her, felt a sick sensation and a rush of nervous energy. *Don't look down and don't think about it*, she told herself firmly. And then she pulled herself back up into position and shook off her fears, focused on looking at the track ahead of her.

She was in sync with the grey horse's gallop now, moving with him, staying low over his neck, crouching like a jockey. As they rounded the first corner her arms were beginning to ache, feeling the strain of holding the stallion back. Avery had told her not to push Angel too hard, but she wasn't pushing at all – she was using every bit of strength she had just to hold him!

Issie's fingers were cramping from holding the reins so tight, the leather cutting into her fingers. Now, as she came past the trees that marked halfway on the course, she loosened her grip a little and Angel instantly took the bit and lengthened his stride. He was still fighting her hands, asking for even more rein, wanting to go faster.

"You want to go, huh, boy?" Issie whispered to him. She loosened the reins off more this time. She wasn't going to fight him any more. "OK, Angel," she said, letting the reins go slack, "time to go!"

As the great, grey stallion began to really lengthen his stride and extend his neck, Issie felt the wind in her face, blowing dust into her eyes, blurring her vision. She tried to stay low so that the horse's mane protected her, and focused all her energy into hanging on as they headed down the final stretch.

As they crossed the line, Issie saw Avery out of the corner of her eye, clicking his stopwatch. He looked pleased. Angel, meanwhile, was thrilling at the chance to run, so much so that it took Issie another few hundred metres before she could pull the stallion back to a trot and turn him round to return to her instructor.

"Well?" she said to Tom. "How did we do?"

Avery showed Issie the numbers on the stopwatch. "He just did two kilometres in two minutes twenty. Never mind the Silver Bridle," he said, "we should be entering Angel at Ascot."

Over the next two days Avery and Issie trained Angel at the fields. Avery would get her to gallop the horse flat out for a lap or two and breeze the horse for a couple more laps of the barren fields, before trotting him for another twenty minutes or so to cool him down.

Every time Issie rode Angel around the track, she felt more and more in the groove with the grey stallion beneath her. When Avery had first shortened her stirrups so that she was riding high in the saddle she had felt a little unstable, out of balance. Now, it felt like the most natural thing in the world to be perched up there on top of this enormous horse, feeling the wind biting into her face as the stallion ran at a gallop towards the finish line.

On the Thursday, Francoise and Alfie accompanied them to the training grounds. Francoise wore a shotgun at her hip and Alfie carried a length of white rope slung over his shoulder.

"What's that for?" Issie asked.

"You want Angel to be fast at the break, don't you?" Francoise replied. "Well, this is how they start the horses for the Silver Bridle. There will be a length of white rope strung across the square. The horses will line up behind it and then when the starter's gun goes they will take off. That is what we will now practise."

And so Issie spent the morning lining Angel up again and again behind the white rope while Avery and Francoise held each end. Alfie stood nearby with the shotgun and fired it into the air every time Francoise and Avery dropped the rope. At exactly the same moment, Issie dug her heels into Angel's sides, urging the stallion forward.

"We want him to make the connection between the gun firing and the rope falling so that he leaps forward on cue," Avery explained. And so they kept going, starting the horse over and over again, firing the gun and dropping the rope, honing his instincts so that after a dozen or so times, Issie didn't even need to kick him on, the stallion instinctively surged forward the moment the rope fell. By the end of the day all four of them were convinced that when the race day came, Angel would be the fastest horse at the break. Now all he had to do was stay in front.

"How is the training progressing?" Roberto asked them at dinner that evening. "Do we have a champion in our stables?"

Avery pushed his fork into his paella. "I think so," he replied.

"Victorioso will be the horse to beat," Roberto continued. "The black stallion is a threat, especially with Vega on his back."

"Angel can take Victorioso," Avery said with certainty. "He's fast, Roberto. Faster than any Andalusian has the right to be. When the race starts he'll be out in front. Issie just has to keep him there."

"Do not forget, you must be careful on the corners," Alfie told Issie. "The village square isn't built like a real race track. The turns are much sharper than they look."

"He's right," Francoise agreed. "The square is white chalk underfoot and very slippery. It is not uncommon for horses to slide and crash, and the houses are built so close to the streets if the horses don't stay on course they risk slamming into the walls."

"OK," Issie said nervously. "I'll be careful on the corners."

Roberto shook his head. "It is just as dangerous on the straight. There, the riders will try and grab you, your clothes, your reins, anything they can get their hands on. They will try and unbalance you, try and pull you off your horse so that they can get past you."

"Isn't that illegal?" Issie asked.

"Nothing is illegal in this race," said Roberto. "On the day of the Silver Bridle the village square will become a battleground. Do you truly think you are ready for that?"

Issie put down her fork. Suddenly she didn't feel so hungry any more. The race was coming and nothing could stop it now. Was she ready? She had to be.

Chapter 14

The next morning, when Issie sat down to breakfast with Avery, he told her that the training session was cancelled for the day.

"He's already race-fit and you've learnt every trick I have to show you," Avery said. "Why don't you just saddle him up and go off for a ride, just the two of you? Don't gallop him, just take him for a bit of a hack. Relax, get your head together."

Issie was happy to be left to her own devices. Last night's discussion of tactics at the dinner table had left her a bundle of nerves. Going for a ride by herself was the perfect way to calm down and mentally prepare herself for tomorrow's race.

At the stables, the grey stallion gave a nicker as she

walked into his stall, greeting Issie as if she were an old friend. The training over the past few days had made Issie even more aware of how special Angel really was. She loved his softness, how he could be so strong and focused when he raced, and yet so gentle here in the stables. In the afternoons, while El Caballo *vaqueros* were having their siestas, Issie would often come by to visit Angel. She would sit down in the straw at the side of his stall and chat away to the stallion as if he were Stella or Kate, talking to him about everything she was thinking, about how much she missed Storm, and about her life back in Chevalier Point with Blaze and Comet.

Sitting there next to the majestic stallion she felt completely safe, despite the fact that with a single sweep of his mighty hooves he could have struck her a mortal blow. She wasn't afraid. Angel was the gentlest horse she had ever met, unlike any other stallion she had ever encountered. The horse, for his part, seemed glad of her company. He would cock one ear as he listened to her idle chatter and then, if he got bored with Issie's endless stories, he would lower his neck, nudging the girl with his muzzle, which was his signal that he wanted her to scratch him in the sweet spot just behind his ears.

"No training today, Angel," Issie told the grey stallion

as she saddled him up. "We've got the day o—
to take a ride, just you and me."

The sky was clear and blue, and the early-morning sun was already warm on her bare skin as Issie rode into the cobbled courtyard. Beneath her, Angel was keyed up and ready to gallop, and she had to steady him back with her legs and her hands.

"Not today, boy," she cooed to the horse. "Save it for tomorrow, today we're just going to take it easy."

They cantered out through the gates of El Caballo Danza Magnifico and Issie was about to turn left towards the olive-tree hills and the race track, but something made her change her mind. Instead, she turned right, back around the white walls of the hacienda, through the fields where the mares and their foals were grazing, heading towards the gorge.

"We're not going all the way to Vega's," she reassured Angel, "I just want to go to the end of the gorge."

Once they had entered the gorge Issie held Angel to a trot, careful not to let him injure himself on the rocky terrain. She looked at the chalky cliffs rising up on either side of her, the slit of blue sky above her head.

...that Vega's men had ...hacienda to this gorge when ...colt back. So much had happened ... Throughout it all, though, Issie had never ...why she had come here. She was here to get her ...back. Now, as she rode on through the gorge, she realised she was riding towards Vega's hacienda, drawn towards the colt once more. She knew she couldn't get close enough to see him without getting caught, but she wished she could, just for a moment. She wanted to let him know that she hadn't forgotten him, that she was doing her best to get him back.

"Just one more day, Storm," she said under her breath, "one more day and you'll be with me again, I promise."

She was lost in her own thoughts as she trotted Angel on, heading into the narrow part of the gorge, a skinny path cut between the rocks, and it took her a moment to realise that there was a shadow in front of them, and it was moving towards them at speed.

She could see that it was a rider on horseback, but the sunlight was behind whoever it was, and the light was so strong it blinded her. It wasn't until they were much closer that she could make out who it was. The horse was an enormous black stallion – and the rider was none other than Miguel Vega.

Seized with panic, Issie tried to turn Angel round, but they were in the narrowest part of the gorge and turning here was impossible. She was in a frenzy now, trying to rein-back to get away, when she heard Vega's voice calling out to her.

"Wait! Do not run, little girl. I want to talk to you."

And then she was face to face with Vega, the man grinning stupidly at her, his bushy moustache twitching with pleasure at her obvious discomfort.

"The young *señorita*!" Vega said. "You came looking for me? What a lovely surprise!"

Issie felt her heart racing. "I wasn't looking for you." She tried to keep the fear out of her voice but she knew that Vega would be able to see that she was shaking. "Let me leave – I want to go home."

"Ah," Vega said. "You are afraid of Miguel Vega? Do not be scared. I only want to talk! It is fortunate that we have met here today. Why not take advantage of this wonderful opportunity that now presents itself to both of us?" His voice was as oily as his slicked-back hair. "I hear that Marius is injured and that you are the one who will now be riding against my hacienda in the Silver Bridle."

Issie nodded.

Vega smiled. "Excellent! Then luck is truly on your side, because this meeting may be most beneficial to you."

"What do you mean?" Issie was getting nervous. She had her hands and legs poised, ready to manoeuvre Angel quickly back in a half-circle to gallop off if she needed to, if Vega got any closer. Angel was ready to run too. He hated being this close to Vega, and Issie could feel the stallion's muscles twitching with barely controlled desperation to get away from the bully who had inflicted the pain of the *serreta* upon him so long ago.

The mustachioed man laughed and the fat on his belly wobbled beneath his cummerbund. "Look at you! As tense as a cat! Do not fear. I have no plans to hurt you…" A malevolent grin played across his face. "Why would I? I do not need to. Not when I still have your colt."

Issie's eyes widened in horror. "What do you mean? Is that a threat? What have you done to him?"

"I have not done anything to him… yet," Vega said. "What happens to him next is up to you."

Vega rode the black stallion a few steps closer, and Issie fought to control Angel as the grey stallion became more desperate than ever to get away from the man he hated so deeply. "Hold your horse still and listen," Vega snapped, "because I am making you an offer that you have no choice but to accept. I do not want to take any chances with the contest tomorrow. If you agree to hold Angel back, and make sure that you lose the race, then I will be generous. I will give you back your colt and you will be free to take him home. You have my word."

"You want me to lose?" Issie said.

"Oh, I am sure I will beat you anyway," Vega said boastfully. "Miguel Vega is a great rider. My horse Victorioso is magnificent. A little girl like you, a *chica*, you will never beat us. But then I figure, why take chances? I want your word that you will lose. I look forward to seeing the face of Roberto Nunez when you come in last."

"So if I lose the race, you'll give me back my colt."

"*Si*, *si*, of course," Vega said dismissively, "but you must not try to pass me in the race. If you try to take the lead at any stage I will know that you have betrayed me. My men will be watching you too and they will know that this is the signal to return to my stables and fix the *serreta* bridle on to your beloved colt. If you cross the line first, your colt will suffer for it. You must bow to my demands. It is the only way to save your beloved Nightstorm."

"How do I know you'll really give him back to me?" Issie asked.

"You have Miguel Vega's word as a gentleman," Vega

said. As he said this, he rode a step closer towards her and suddenly reached out a hand to grasp at Angel's reins. The stallion was too quick for him, though, rearing back and pirouetting on his hocks. All the time they had been talking, Issie had been inching the stallion backwards slowly. They had now reached a small gap in the rocks that was wide enough to turn and she did so now.

"Run then!" Vega laughed after her as Angel broke into a gallop. "But do not forget my kind offer. If you do not take it you are nothing but a fool, and your precious Storm, your colt, will suffer."

Vega made no attempt to chase after them. As he had already told Issie, he didn't need to hurt her. Not when he could cause her so much more pain by hurting the thing she loved most – her colt.

Issie spoke to no one about her encounter with Vega when she got back to El Caballo. She knew what Avery and Roberto would both say if she told them. They would tell her that Vega was not a man to be trusted, that even if she lost the race on purpose as he asked, he would not honour the deal. Her best hope still, they would say, was to win the race and get Storm back.

Issie knew this was probably true. But Storm was her baby, and if she won the race now it would be as if she were the one putting the *serreta* on him herself. It would be her fault when Vega's men strapped the spiked metal noseband to the colt's face and scarred him forever.

It was easy for Issie to excuse herself from dinner that night. Everyone expected her to have nerves the night before the race. She had stayed upstairs in her room, fretting about the decision that she was about to make. She realised now that even if she threw the race Vega would not give Storm back, and yet she could no more abandon her colt than she could betray El Caballo Danza Magnifico. It was the hardest choice she had ever had to make.

It was almost midnight. Dinner had been eaten and Francoise, Avery and Roberto were still gathered in the library talking tactics when Issie turned up with her pillow and her duvet.

"I thought I'd sleep in the stables tonight," she explained. "I want to keep an eye on Angel."

Francoise nodded at this. "I understand. My cot bed that I use when the mares are foaling is folded away in the tack room. It is easy to set up, you can put it in Angel's stall. Why don't you go and make yourself comfortable out there and let me bring you some dinner? I got the chef to keep a platter for you in case you were hungry after all."

Issie shook her head. "I don't want anything to eat, thanks, Francoise. I'll be fine."

"Then we'll see you in the morning. We leave for the village at seven." Francoise smiled gently at her.

"OK, see you then," Issie said.

"Goodnight Issie. Try and get some sleep out there, OK?" Avery said.

"I will," Issie said.

She wasn't certain that she would get any sleep, though. After the meeting with Vega today she was now worried that his men might try to sneak into the stables and hurt Angel during the night. She would put nothing past Vega – no dirty tactics were beneath this man. She would be sleeping with one eye open, looking out for trouble.

Angel greeted her with a nicker as she arrived in his stall with her bedding and the cot bed from the tack shed tucked under her arm.

"It's OK, boy," she said gently to the grey stallion. "It's just me. I thought I'd come and share your stall for the night."

Angel was happy to have a room-mate. But he could

sense that something was wrong. Issie usually lavished attention on him, but tonight she just sat on the edge of her cot staring out into the night. She looked like she had the weight of the world on her shoulders.

Issie sat up on guard duty for a couple of hours. Then she began to think that maybe this was part of Vega's master plan. He had her worried sick when she should be sleeping! If she didn't get some sleep tonight then she would be too exhausted to race tomorrow anyway.

She took one last look out of the stable door. There was no one around. She lay down on the camp bed and discovered that it was surprisingly comfy. The night air was warm, but she still tucked the duvet around her. In the stall next to her Angel stirred, moving his hooves in the straw.

"G'night Angel," Issie said drowsily. She fell asleep almost straight away, and it wasn't long before the dream began.

It was one of the strangest dreams she'd ever had. She was reliving everything that had happened in the past few weeks: Storm, the race for the Silver Bridle. In her dream it all became clear to her. When she woke up, sitting bolt upright on the camp bed, her heart was racing. Her dream had been the answer! She had figured it out. She knew how to save Storm and she knew exactly what she needed to do. But that wasn't why she had woken up. She was awake because she'd heard a noise in the corridor at the entrance to the stable block. Someone was there!

Angel heard it too. He raised his noble head, his ears pricked forward towards the stable entrance. "Do you hear it too, boy?" Issie asked. There it was! The scraping sound of someone, or something, moving on the cobbled stones. She looked up and saw a shape in the courtyard archway at the entrance of the stables.

"Francoise? Is that you?" Issie called. Perhaps the Frenchwoman had brought her dinner after all? The shadow didn't answer her. It did, however, begin to move, coming closer out of the darkness outside, heading towards the light of the stable loose boxes. "Hello? Who is it?" Issie was trembling now. "Francoise?"

Beside her in the stall, Angel moved about anxiously. She could make out the shape of a shadow moving in the darkness, now coming finally into the light of the stables.

And then suddenly Issie could see quite clearly who it was. The shock was too much for her, and she instantly burst into a flood of tears as she realised that it wasn't Francoise or one of Vega's men. It wasn't a human at all. It was a horse. It was Mystic.

Chapter 15

Tears were streaming down Issie's face as she rushed forward and threw her arms around the grey pony. "Mystic!" She was so choked with emotion she was struggling to get the words out. "Ohmygod! You don't know how glad I am to see you."

Mystic seemed just as pleased to see Issie too. He nickered warmly to her, nuzzling her with his sooty grey muzzle. Issie giggled as he did this, and began to pull herself together. She took a deep breath and used her sleeve to wipe her eyes and dry away the last of her tears.

"Mystic," she said, "I don't know how you got here, but I am so happy you came. Things have been so messed up. I must have fallen asleep because I had this dream…"

She'd woken up suddenly when Mystic had arrived, but

the dream had remained with her, and it was still flashing through her mind now, like a memory of something that really happened, all the details so vivid and real.

"Mystic," she whispered intently to the grey stallion, "I had a dream. And you were in it. You were there and you helped me to save Storm. That's why you're here, isn't it?"

Did she and Mystic share the same dream? Somehow she knew that he understood her completely and he knew what they needed to do.

Issie gave the grey gelding one last stroke on his sleek, dappled neck. Then she let her hand fall and stood back from her pony. "You have to go now. Until tomorrow, when the race begins," she said. Then she added cryptically, "You know I can't help you. You have to do it alone. You have to go and get him. I'm relying on you, OK?"

Mystic seemed to understand. He turned away from her and trotted back the way he had come, towards the entrance of the stables. When he reached the archway he stopped for a moment, silhouetted in the half light, his dark eyes shining as he stared back at Issie.

Then suddenly he wheeled about on his hocks, his silver tail flowing out behind him as he turned and cantered off across the courtyard. And then he was gone. As quickly as he had arrived in the stables here at El Caballo he had disappeared once more. Issie stood for a moment longer, staring out into the darkness. Was she right about this? Issie felt certain that she was connected somehow with the grey pony, that both of them had shared the same vision, and that Mystic would act when the time was right tomorrow and play his part. He wouldn't fail her.

Issie stood a moment longer, staring at the dark night outside. Then she turned round and walked back to the stall where Angel was craning his neck over the chain. He had seen Mystic too and he was wondering what was going on. Issie put out a hand and stroked the grey stallion's forelock.

"Not much longer now," she said to the stallion. Soon enough it would be dawn and the race for the Silver Bridle would begin. Now that Mystic was here, though, everything had changed. For the first time, as she stood there, Issie felt a surge of excitement at the thought of riding Angel in the race. A few moments ago she'd been in despair, but now she had a plan.

"It's going to be OK, Angel," she said to the big grey stallion standing next to her. "Mystic is here. And we're going to win."

Alfie! Wake up!" It was before dawn back at the hacienda and Issie was in Alfie's room shaking his shoulder gently. "Alfie!" she hissed. The shaking was not so gentle now as she gave him a shove and Alfie sat bolt upright in bed.

"*Madre Mia*! What's going on? Issie? What are you doing in my room?"

"Alfie, shhh, I have to ask you something," Issie said. "Listen, I need your help. I know a way to get Storm back. Vega has asked me to throw the race—"

"Vega? Throw the race? Issie, you can't—" Alfie began.

"Shhh!" Issie said. "I have a plan, but I'm going to need your help. You have to trust me, OK? I can't explain everything, but you have to trust me. Now are you in?"

Alfie took a deep breath and looked hard at Issie as if he were trying to make up his mind. Finally he spoke. "Of course I'm in," he said. "Tell me what I have to do."

The pounding rhythm of the Spanish flamenco filled the air as Issie, Avery, Roberto and Francoise rode towards the village that morning. Everywhere Issie looked, red roses littered the ground, trampled on the cobblestones beneath the horses' hooves. There were brightly coloured banners hanging from the windows of all the buildings. The sound of Spanish castanets and the joyous shouts of the supporters filled the air as the fans lined the streets leading to the village, all waiting to cheer on the jockeys from their favourite hacienda.

Twelve haciendas would compete here today and each of them was determined to outdo the others. Their rivalry began with the grooming and presentation of their horses. The spectators from each hacienda were on horseback and all dressed up in their team colours. Most splendid of all, though, were the twelve racehorses from each of the competing stables. Their manes were plaited with ribbons and bobbles in the colours of their hacienda and streamers were braided into their tails. The jockeys too were dressed in colourful and theatrical costumes. Each of them wore racing silks in hacienda colours that matched their horse's braids.

"I feel silly in this outfit," Issie grumbled as she rolled up the sleeves of her jockey silks. The silks were striped in the red, orange and violet colours of El Caballo Danza Magnifico, with a letter C and a red heart in the centre on Issie's back. "This shirt is too big for me."

"They were Alfie's silks," Francoise said. "I didn't

have time to alter them." She looked around. "Where is Alfie? He said he was going to catch us up. He'll miss the race at this rate."

"Ummm," Issie said, "I wouldn't worry about him. He said to tell you that he had something to do back at the stables. He'll be here later."

Now they passed the fountain that marked the entrance to the village square and Issie could see the track that they would race on, the sides of the streets swarming with people, waiting to cheer on their own hacienda.

As she looked down the wide white chalk streets of the square Issie knew exactly what lay ahead of her. This wasn't a game, it was real. Today she would be risking her life to win, riding against men twice her size and twice her age.

"Are you nervous?" asked Avery.

Issie didn't know what to say. This morning when she'd been telling Alfie her plan, she hadn't been nervous in the least. She'd been so certain that her idea would work. But in the harsh light of day, she was still a young girl, mounting up to ride against eleven men in a dangerous horse race that pitted riders against each other in a rough and tumble contest with no rules.

"Just remember our game plan," Avery said. "You've got to be away fast at the break, get out in front so that the other riders can't get near you. If they can't touch you then you can't be shoved around. Just keep Angel ahead of the pack and stay in the lead. He's got the speed to hold them off and the stamina to last the distance. Be careful taking the corners and then, on the third lap, when you're coming around to the final stretch, you can loosen the reins and really let him go, urge him on over the finish line."

Issie looked at her instructor, wondering how to explain what she was about to tell him. "That's just the thing, Tom, about our race strategy. I want to—"

The loud parp of a horn interrupted her.

"This is it!" Roberto said. "Time for you to line up." He looked at Issie and smiled. "I know you will ride your best for El Caballo Danza Magnifico. And that is all I ask. I am proud that you are riding for our stables, Isadora – you take with you the hopes and dreams for our future. Good luck, my brave friend."

He put out his hand and Issie shook it. It felt quite odd, shaking Roberto's hand. She had puzzled all morning about whether she should try to explain her plan to Roberto. Now, at the last minute, she decided that Roberto needed to know what was really going on.

"Roberto, I have to tell you," Issie began, "Alfie and I have this plan. Vega, he told me that—"

"*Vaqueros*!" A voice over the loudspeaker interrupted her. The announcer was saying something in Spanish.

"The race is about to begin. It is time for you to take your position at the start line now," Roberto said. "We will have time to talk later…"

He gestured to Francoise, who dismounted and handed the reins of her horse to Roberto, and then took Angel by the reins and led Issie over to join the other horses behind the white rope.

"What is it?" Francoise asked. "What were you trying to tell Roberto about Vega? Is it something about the race?"

Issie shook her head. "It's nothing," she said. She realised there was no point in talking about it now. They wouldn't understand. How could they when they didn't know about Mystic? Besides, the race was about to be run. Issie's plan was about to unfold. They would all see soon enough.

All this time, despite the noise, the crowds and the flags, Angel had been his good-natured self, as calm as ever. The grey stallion had been perfectly behaved on the way here and his manners had been impeccable as Issie rode him around the village square. But now, as they came back to the fountain where they would line up to begin the race, Angel's mood suddenly changed. The horse had spied Miguel Vega in the crowd ahead of them, sitting astride Victorioso, his mighty black stallion. At the sight of Vega, Angel's stride stiffened and he began to skip nervously, crab-stepping sideways beneath Issie, reluctant to step forward towards the start line.

"Easy, Angel," Issie soothed him. "Steady, Angel," she said firmly. Angel was trembling at the very sight of Vega. Luckily, Issie didn't have to line up right next to him. Two other riders from rival stables were positioned in the line between her and Vega, but that didn't stop the mustachioed man from leaning over in full view of everyone and taunting her.

"Remember my kind offer, little girl! We have a deal!" Vega called to her. Francoise looked up at Issie, confusion and shock on her face. "What is he talking about, Isadora? A deal? You bargained with Vega?" Her voice was stricken with panic.

Issie ignored Vega's taunt and his grinning face and looked down at Francoise. "Don't worry, Francoise. I can't explain now, but—"

"Issie… has he threatened you?" Francoise asked. "Listen to me! Vega is not to be trusted. What did he say to you?"

"Francoise… I—" Issie wanted to explain, but before she had the chance to finish the sentence there was another loud honk of the horn, signalling that the grooms had to let go of the horses now, and leave the jockeys to line up alone behind the rope, ready to start the race.

Francoise gave Issie one last, long pleading look and let go of Angel's reins and walked away. Issie watched her go. She wished she could have told Francoise, but there just wasn't time. The race was about to begin.

Issie took a tighter grip on Angel's reins and stood up in the stirrups of her saddle, ready for the rope to drop and the break to come. Above the sounds of the flamenco and the clacking of the castanets she could hear a louder rhythm, the sound of her heart pounding in her chest. She was about to risk everything and she knew it, about to turn her back on everything that she had agreed to with Tom and ride a different race, the race of her life. She hoped she was ready for it.

Beneath her, she felt Angel tense every muscle in his body, the rope pulling taut across his chest as the horses all lined up next to each other ready to run.

"On your marks," the voice on the sidelines shouted, "get set... go!"

The pistol sounded and the rope dropped. As the horses broke, Issie remembered Tom's advice. Get out in front of the rest of the pack and stay at the front. Ride in the lead and that way no one can touch you or try to hurt you. It was good advice – under normal circumstances. But Issie wasn't riding under normal circumstances. When the rope fell away, instead of letting Angel surge forward at the break as he had been trained to do, she did completely the opposite, holding the stallion back.

Angel tried to lunge forward, fighting hard against her hands. The other horses had taken off and he wanted to join them. He wanted to run! Issie's arms ached from the strain of keeping him back, but she held him firm, allowing the other riders to get a whole length's head start on the grey stallion before she finally loosened her fingers a little, leaned forward in the saddle and let him go.

Up ahead of her, Miguel Vega turned round and flicked a quick nod of approval at her. He could see what she was doing, holding Angel back so that the other riders were now ahead of her. From the sidelines, Roberto and Avery could see it too.

"What on earth is wrong with her?" Avery shouted over the noise of the crowd. "It looked like she was holding Angel back at the break! She's supposed to get to the front! What is she doing?"

Issie was at the back of the field, mixed up with the other straggling riders at the rear, and now she was in danger of precisely the thing that Tom Avery had feared. As the riders jostled and fought for position, Issie felt a hard blow on her shoulder as a jockey to her left riding a big bay stallion shoved her viciously out of his way. Issie let out a shriek, and tried to keep her balance, swerving to avoid the other rider. Then she pulled back hard on Angel's reins, forcing the stallion to slow down and drop even further back behind the field. She was now right at the tail of the race, the very last horse, trailing the leaders by almost eight lengths as they came around the square and back towards the fountain that would mark the end of the first lap.

"What is she doing?" Avery said again as Issie rode past them. Instead of focusing on the track, Issie seemed to be paying no attention to the race! She was staring out distractedly over the buildings, looking out towards El Caballo Danza Magnifico.

"She has lost her nerve," Roberto said. "She is too afraid to ride past them!"

As he said this, he caught sight of Francoise, who was running back to join them, pushing her way through the crowds to reach them. When she finally reached them she was exhausted, panting for breath as she tried to speak. "It's Issie…" she said, "… I think something is terribly wrong! I think Vega has got to her and threatened Storm."

"What do you mean?" Avery said.

"Look at her!" Francoise replied. "Don't you see? He's using the colt to blackmail her. That is why she is riding like this."

Francoise took a deep breath and the words came tumbling out. "Tom, I think she's losing on purpose. I think Issie is going to throw the race!"

Chapter 16

As Issie grappled with the stallion, holding him back, she caught sight of Avery, Francoise and Roberto watching her with disbelief from the sidelines. It felt awful to do this to them. Issie only hoped that her plan would work and she would have the chance to explain once the race was done.

Francoise had been right, of course, when she said that Issie was losing the race on purpose. She was holding Angel back, staying at the very rear of the field, letting Vega stay in the lead. It was all part of Issie's plan. She had to make Vega believe that she was really going to throw the race.

Issie knew Vega was not to be trusted, but she had no doubt that he meant it when he threatened to put the *serreta* on Storm. She knew he wasn't bluffing when he told her that if she got out in front, he would signal one of his men to return to the stables and put the metal-barbed bridle on the colt. And so she was going to hold Angel back until the time was right to strike. She had to let Vega keep his lead, for Storm's sake.

Beneath her now, as they came around to the end of the first lap, Angel snorted his objections. He had been straining on the reins since the break, and Issie could feel the leather cutting deep into her fingers as she gripped with all her strength to keep the horse back. Up ahead of her she could see the other riders. Vega was at the front of the field on Victorioso. He was at least ten lengths ahead of her now and there were ten horses between them. Issie needed to act soon, to put her plan into play. But right now she had no choice but to hang back. Vega's men were watching her suspiciously. Vega had told them to keep an eye on her. When she made her move, so would they. Timing was everything and so she had no choice but to hang on to the reins, try to ignore the pain in her fingers and wait. As she came around the village square this time she had a clear view to El Caballo and she looked down at the gates, hoping to see the signal she was waiting for. Her heart sank – there was no signal.

"Come on, Mystic!" Issie muttered to herself. "I'm depending on you. Where are you?"

Mystic, meanwhile, was galloping as if his life depended on it, racing across the green fields where the mares grazed around the white walls of El Caballo Danza Magnifico. The grey gelding wasn't alone. He was matched stride for stride by the leggy, bay colt who ran beside him. It was Storm! His head was held high as he ran for all he was worth, determined to prove that he could keep pace with the grey horse, sticking to Mystic's side like glue as they ran together.

This was Issie's master plan. It had all come to her like a vision in her dream last night just before Mystic had appeared.

Mystic was the answer. Issie couldn't save Storm. But Mystic could. While Issie was at the village taking part in the race, Mystic could go to Vega's hacienda, help Storm to escape, and bring him home. Mystic would be the one to rescue the colt – on his own.

The race created the perfect opportunity. Vega's men were all at the village square and the stables were deserted. There was no one watching the colt, Nightstorm was alone and unguarded. When Mystic arrived at the hacienda there wasn't a soul waiting to stop him.

Storm had gone mad with excitement when he saw the grey pony. It had been a simple matter for Mystic to encourage the colt to follow him by jumping over the five-bar gate. Storm had taken the fence just as easily as the paddock gate that he was only too accustomed to jumping back home.

The two horses had clattered down the cobbled stables, and straight out of the front gates as Mystic led Storm through the orange grove and across the pastures, towards the gorge.

All they had to do now was make it through the gates of El Caballo Danza Magnifico. Issie needed to be sure they were safe. She planned to win this race, but not until she was certain that her colt was truly home and free from the clutches of Miguel Vega.

That was where Alfie came in. He was a crucial part of her plan. Alfie would look out for Storm and signal to Issie the moment that the colt had arrived at the stables by running the El Caballo flag up the flagpole. The flag was the signal. Issie would see it flying and know that she was free to give Angel his head and try to win the race.

That was the plan. So far, Issie had carried it out perfectly. She had stayed at the back of the field, making it look like she was completely willing to lose this race, waiting until she was certain that Mystic's mission had been successful and the colt was safe at home at El Caballo again.

It was a good plan, but time was tight. Would Mystic get the colt back in time? Would she see Alfie's signal? She needed to know that Mystic's mission had been a success and that she could go ahead and try to win back this race – before it was too late.

As the crowds cheered around the village square, Issie kept holding Angel back at the rear of the other riders. They had turned the corner now to begin the second lap, and as she rode back around the square past the fountain, she could see down over the tops of the village houses once more with a clear view to El Caballo Danza Magnifico nestled in the valley below.

"Come on, Mystic!" Issie muttered. "We're out of time."

And then she caught sight of a vision that made her heart leap. A golden flag with a red heart was being raised up the pole so that it fluttered in the breeze. It was the signal! They had done it! Storm was home.

The sight of the flag was all that Issie needed to spur

her on. She felt a sudden chill run through her. Vega and Victorioso were still out in front and they must have been at least eight lengths ahead of her. She hoped she hadn't blown it. Had she left it too late to make her move? Too late to win?

On the sidelines, Avery, Roberto and Francoise were thinking the same thing. "She has lost," Roberto said. "Francoise is right. I think she has thrown the race on purpose."

"Issie wouldn't do that!" Avery snapped.

"No?" Roberto said. "Then how do you explain the way she is riding?"

Francoise kept her eyes on the race. "Even if she tries to claw her way back now," the Frenchwoman said ominously, "I do not believe she can do it. There is too much distance between her and Vega. The race is halfway through. She cannot possibly gain the distance on him in time to win."

At the back of the field, though, Issie was about to try and do exactly that. As soon as she'd come up with her plan she'd known she would have to win this race from the back, and not from the start. She had never been expecting to lead the pack. Instead, she'd known she would have to hold Angel and wait until Storm was safe, until the right moment to strike. And she knew she could do it. She had faith in the enormous speed of the horse she was riding.

"OK, Angel." She leaned down low on the grey stallion's neck and finally released the reins that she had been gripping so tightly since the race began. "Time to go, boy."

Angel, who had been leaning on Issie's hands, desperate to free himself since the very start of the race, responded instantly. He surged forward, his stride lengthening, making up the distance between himself and the horses at the very back of the tight-knit pack within just a few lengths.

The horses ahead of her all slowed down as they reached the treacherous corner turn, and Issie did the same, slowing Angel back just enough to make it around without skidding. She didn't want to risk sliding her horse into the crowds and the café tables that lined the streets of the square. As soon as she was back on the straight, though, she sped up again, asking Angel gallop harder. By the time they came around to the last corner of the second lap, Angel had caught up to the other stragglers. There were four riders grouped together at the rear in front of Issie. They were riding together in a tight knot, blocking Issie's path so that she couldn't get through. Angel had to slow down, settling in behind the pack for a moment as Issie decided on her next move. The safest thing to do would be to ride wide on the track, to go to the outside of the horses and ride around them. But Issie wasn't interested in the safest route, she was interested in the fastest. She pulled hard on the stallion's right rein and guided him to the inside, towards the small gap near the metal rails. She was going to pass through the gap, squeezing inside of the horses who were running ahead of them. She didn't have the luxury of time. The inside track was fastest and they would simply have to fight their way to get through.

"What is she trying to do?" Francoise screamed from the sidelines now. "She is riding through the other riders, she will get herself killed."

"No, she won't!" Avery yelled over the noise of the crowd. "She's making her move now, she knows what she's doing!"

As Angel made a dive for the gap, Issie looked to her left and saw the jockey on the horse beside her give her a filthy look. He wasn't about to be overtaken by a girl!

He had ridden the Silver Bridle before and he knew there were no rules in this race. He lifted his stick, ready to strike out at her, but before he could swing his blow Issie had ducked out of the way, bending down even lower in the saddle to sweep past as she clucked Angel on, kicking the grey stallion lightly with her heels to ask for more speed. The other jockey was left open-mouthed in her wake.

"Did you see that?" Francoise squeaked. "She is too small and quick. They cannot lay a hand on her. She is beating them at their own game!"

Now the grey stallion put on a surge of speed, his powerful haunches beginning to come into play, working to propel him to even greater strides. He raced past the next two horses as if they weren't even there, ducking and weaving his way through the field as Issie guided him on fearlessly. They were halfway through the horses now, in sixth place, as they approached the line for the third lap.

As they crossed the line for the third and final lap, Issie saw they were coming up towards a treacherous corner again. Angel was in full gallop and going far too fast to make it safely around the bend. Issie had to ignore the pain in her fingers and pull back on the reins with all her strength, fighting to get the stallion back under control and slow him down. She lost a little ground, but she knew it was the right thing to do, they had to make it safely round the corner.

Then disaster struck right in front of her. A rider had kept his mount going at full gallop, taking a risk that he would still somehow make it round the corner. He hadn't. His horse skidded into the pavement, knocking chairs and tables aside, and the crowd began to scatter to get out of the way. There was screaming and shouting as the horse crashed through a hawker's stall, trying to regain its footing. The horse's hooves scrabbled across the cobbled pavements and the jockey was flung out of the saddle and crashed to the ground.

Before anyone could help him, a second horse skidded at the same corner, also going far too fast, and got tangled in the fray.

The crowd immediately gathered around the horses and riders, trying to help them back to their feet. The horses were both standing up, their flanks heaving, the whites of their eyes rolling back from the fright. They were unharmed, but the crash meant they were well and truly out of the race.

"Get off the track!" Issie yelled as she galloped straight for them. She was still in this race and the people who were trying to help were now blocking her path!

"Out of the way! *Vamos*!" she shouted. The crowds scattered off the street just in time as she turned the corner with expert precision and raced on past. With these two horses eliminated there were only another two riders left standing between her and Vega. She was bearing down on them fast, and had tightened the gap. Less than four lengths separated her from the leader now.

Stride by stride, Angel was gaining on the other horses. As they came around the last corner of the third lap, heading into the final stretch, Issie knew it was time. She began to ride Angel like a race jockey, just as Avery had shown her, urging the horse on with her hands, talking constantly to the great, grey stallion, asking him to give her more. Angel was listening to her – he stretched out even further, sweeping over the ground with huge strides. He passed the other two horses in front of him as if they were standing still. Now, as they came into the final stretch, there was only Vega between them and the finish line.

"She will never take him. Victorioso is too fast and Vega is too clever to be beaten in the home straight," Francoise said.

Avery shook his head. "Issie can take him," he said. "Just watch her."

Out on the track, Issie was riding for all she was worth. Her head was tucked down low over Angel's neck as she kept talking to the grey stallion, asking him for more, asking him to edge up, stride by stride, chipping away at the gigantic black horse's lead. She knew Angel had the speed in him to take Victorioso. More than that, she knew the grey stallion had the courage, the will, to beat Miguel Vega.

As Angel began to pull up alongside Victorioso, Issie saw surprise on Vega's face. He hadn't been expecting this. And he hadn't been expecting what happened next.

The two horses, Victorioso and Angel, were neck and neck. The two great stallions were racing stride for stride so that Issie and Vega were alongside each other. Vega saw his chance. If this girl was foolish enough to come near him, he was going to make her suffer for it. He lifted one meaty paw from Victorioso's reins, and reached out his arm towards Issie to strike her.

He didn't get the chance. He didn't realise this too was part of Issie's plan. She had been anticipating this moment. In fact, she had been counting on it. She held Angel so that he was racing right next to Victorioso and the grey stallion got a real good look at Vega riding next to him.

At the sight of his enemy, Angel gave a snort of indignation and surged forward in a fresh burst of unmatchable speed that took him ahead of the black stallion. In two lightning strides Angel was out in front of Victorioso, leaving Vega in the dust behind him impotently shaking his fist as Issie catapulted into the lead.

All around them the crowd erupted in wild cheers and shouts, and flowers flew through the air as Issie and Angel passed the fountain for the third and final time and crossed the finish line. They had won.

Chapter 17

Two days after the Silver Bridle had been won, Issie faced yet another test.

As she stood in front of a line of the most beautiful horses she had ever seen she really didn't know if she could do it. They were all so stunning! How could she possibly choose one?

"Hurry up, girl!" A voice from behind her snapped angrily. Issie turned round to see Miguel Vega, dabbing furiously with his hanky at his chubby face as the beads of sweat trickled from beneath his *vaquero* hat.

"Don't rush me!" Issie grinned back at him. She stepped forward and walked down the row of horses until she reached a grey colt. He was a three-year-old Andalusian, with strong conformation, a well-shaped neck and a perfectly dished nose.

Issie looked back at Roberto. "What do you think?"

Roberto nodded. "An excellent choice, Isadora. This young stallion is the son of Victorioso, and his dam is one of Vega's favourite mares. I have long admired this horse and would love to have him in my stables." He smiled. "However, it is your decision."

Issie smiled back at Roberto, and then she reached out a hand and stroked the grey stallion on his pretty dished nose.

"We'll take this one!" she said.

Vega reluctantly signalled his men to lead the stallion away with the others.

"He's hating every moment of this," Avery muttered to Issie with a grin.

"Good!" Issie giggled back.

Vega had been forced to stand there this morning and watch helplessly as Issie, Roberto, Alfie and Francoise each picked a horse from his magnificent herd to take away with them back to El Caballo Danza Magnifico.

Since Issie had won the race for the Silver Bridle, she, along with Roberto, Alfie, Avery and Francoise, had been working her way around the eleven rival haciendas. At every stud farm, they had chosen five of the best horses to take as their prize. Vega's was the last of the eleven haciendas, and now that it was his turn to endure the claiming of the spoils of the Silver Bridle he wasn't liking the process one bit.

"Come on!" he snapped. "You have one left to choose. Make it quick. I do not wish to stand here all day!"

Roberto turned to face Vega now and his smile faded.

"We will not be choosing a fifth horse from you, Miguel."

"What?"

"You heard me," Roberto said. "We have chosen four of your horses today. The fifth horse is the colt that we already have back at our stables."

Vega looked at him suspiciously. "I don't understand."

"Nightstorm is Isadora's colt and you know it. We know you stole him from her. He was never yours to own in the first place. But, as a sign of goodwill, we are willing to let him count for your stables as one of the five horses you owe us."

Vega smiled at this. It seemed like a good deal as far as he was concerned. He had been furious when he had arrived home after losing the race only to discover the colt was missing from the stables. Vega figured one of his men must have foolishly left the gate open, and had given him up for lost until he discovered the colt was back at El Caballo. Now, to be offered this deal was a stroke of good fortune.

"There is a condition, though," Roberto continued. "We are doing this for one reason, pure and simple. We do not want you to have any claim over Storm. The colt will always bear the brand of your stables, but he is not your colt and you know it. He belongs to Isadora. And I am warning you now, if you ever touch him again, if you ever try to steal him or hurt him in any way, as a man of honour I shall be forced to deal with you myself. Am I making myself clear?"

Vega's smile crumpled. "Miguel Vega agrees to your terms," he spat back. "You have your deal, Roberto. And you have my horses. Leave now and let this be the end of all our dealings!"

"With pleasure," Roberto grinned. He turned again to look at Miguel as they left the hacienda. "See you in another ten years, Miguel!"

There was much talk about the horses they had chosen on the way home. Issie was pleased with the young grey stallion that she was leading beside her. Roberto had picked Victorioso, of course, and the black stallion was certainly a great prize. Francoise had chosen a snow-white mare from the same bloodlines that Angel shared.

"She will be good bloodstock for the future Andalusian herd," she explained.

Alfie had chosen a bay Lusitano foal.

"I think you chose him because he looks just like Storm," Issie smiled.

"Storm is much more handsome," Alfie said. "I can see why he means so much to you."

"I want to thank you again for helping me to get him back," Issie said.

Alfie grinned. "I had the easy job! Running a flag up a pole. I'm just glad that it worked out OK." Then he added in a whisper to Issie, "And maybe one day you'll explain to me exactly what really happened that day. How did you do it, Issie? All I know is that your colt came galloping in through the gates following this little grey horse. As soon as I saw them I raised the flag as you asked, and then when I turned round again – it was like the grey horse had just disappeared. You want to tell me what's going on here?"

Issie smiled back at Alfie. "Maybe one day. Meanwhile, let's just say that I owe you one."

No one, except for Issie, of course, really understood how the colt had managed to make his way back all by himself to El Caballo Danza Magnifico during the race.

Issie had simply pronounced that Storm was super-clever and had obviously found his way to El Caballo stables.

"But it makes no sense," Francoise had puzzled. "Even if Vega did leave the gate open and he got loose, how could he possibly know the way here on his own? He has never been here before."

Issie had smiled as she stroked the colt's fluffy bay coat. "I guess it's instinct," she said. "Horses always know the way home."

But where was Nightstorm's true home? Issie had been thinking a lot about that lately, ever since her conversation with Roberto in the training arena that day when he had offered to keep the colt here for her and school him as an El Caballo stallion in the traditional ways of the *haute école*.

Issie knew where her home was. She missed Chevalier Point terribly. She had been away for over two weeks and, even though she knew she would return home to soggy paddocks and muddy, shaggy ponies all pepped up from too much early spring grass, she still longed to be home again now that the excitement was over. She missed Blaze and Comet. She missed her mum. She missed Stella and Kate. To say she even missed Natasha Tucker would have been pushing it, but she was so homesick right now that if Natasha had turned up in Spain at that moment she might even have given her a hug!

Well, she thought, it wasn't long now. They would be home soon. Avery was busy making plans for their travel arrangements. It would be more difficult this time as they needed to transport Storm, so they would be travelling a different route.

"We'll leave tomorrow at midday," Avery told her when they all met in the library that evening for tapas. Issie had grown to love the exotic food. She was nibbling on a shrimp and had loaded her plate with tomato bread, chorizo and slices of Iberian ham. There was Spanish sherry too – a celebration for the adults, although Issie much preferred the fresh orange juice anyway.

"It will be a real pity to see you leave," Roberto told Issie. "I owe you a great debt. I never thought you would win the Silver Bridle and I must apologise for my lack of faith. You are indeed the great rider that Thomas told me you would be, and you are always welcome here at El Caballo Danza Magnifico."

"Thank you, Roberto," Issie said. Then she braced herself and asked the question that had been at the back of her mind ever since she arrived. "If you really owe me a great debt then there's another favour I need to ask of you."

"Certainly," Roberto said. "What is it?"

"Please," Issie said, "I really want to know… who was it that bought Blaze from you and gave her to me?"

Roberto shook his head. "I am afraid I am not at liberty to say. I promised I would never reveal the identity of your benefactor. I owe you a debt, Isadora, but there is someone else who I am even more indebted to—"

"It's OK, Roberto," Avery interrupted him. "It's time to tell her. She deserves to know."

Roberto raised an eyebrow at this. Then he nodded. "So be it. You are her *bonifacio*. It is your decision."

"*Bonifacio*?" Issie was puzzled. It was that word again! The word that Roberto had used when he was talking to Avery that night in the living room. "What does that word mean?" Issie asked.

"It means 'benefactor'," Avery replied. "Issie, it was me. I'm the one who bought Blaze for you."

Issie couldn't believe it. "But Tom, why? How?"

Avery smiled at the astonished look on her face. "Roberto owed me a great favour. Remember, I had saved his life once before. And he had sworn that if he could ever do me a favour, anything I asked for would be mine. I never thought I'd take him up on it, but when I heard about where Blaze was really from, I knew that he would be willing to part with the mare for a fraction of what she was really worth. I knew I could buy her back for you."

"But why did you do it? For me, I mean?" Issie's voice was trembling. She felt as if she was going to cry.

"I guess I blamed myself for what happened when Francoise turned up and you lost Blaze." Avery shook his head. "You had only just recovered from losing Mystic and I was the one who had given Blaze to you. I wanted to make everything better, you see. I thought having a new horse, one like Blaze who really needed you to nurse her back to health, would help you to move on. And I was right, you and Blaze were so perfect for each other. Then, when Francoise arrived to take the mare back, I knew it had broken your heart. It was all my fault. I should never have given you Blaze in the first place. I knew the mare might have been stolen – I just never guessed she was from the famous El Caballo Danza Magnifico."

Roberto interrupted to continue the story. "When Thomas called me, I could not believe it. My old friend, my brother, whom I owed my life to, was calling to collect at last on the great debt I owed him. It made me very happy to let him have Salome. I could never refuse him, of course. And I promised him that I would never tell you who had been your benefactor."

"But why the big secret?" Issie asked.

"I didn't want you to know I'd bought Blaze," Avery said. "I thought your mum would try to pay me back what I had paid for the mare and I didn't want that. I didn't want you to feel that you owed me, because you don't. I was happy to do it. You've got the makings of a great rider, Issie, and I couldn't stand to watch you lose your horse. I lost a horse myself once, and I never really recovered. So I bought Blaze for you. I honestly didn't think I would ever tell you. As time went on, it just seemed easier to keep it a secret. And then when Storm was stolen and Francoise turned up, and we came here, I suppose I realised that I was being unrealistic trying to continue to keep it hidden. You deserve to know," Avery paused. "But I think it's best, don't you, if we keep this between ourselves? I'll tell your mother, of course, when we get home, but I don't really want the whole pony club to know about this. I can do without the kids all queuing up to get their mystery gift ponies from me!"

Issie giggled. "No, I can see that it would be a problem." She looked at her instructor, her eyes shining with tears. "Tom, I am so grateful for what you did for me."

"Don't be," Avery said firmly. "It was something I had to do. For me as much as for you. I'm just glad I could help."

Issie still couldn't believe it. She had come all the way to Spain to get her colt back and she had ended up with so much more. She knew the truth now, the real story behind the mystery benefactor who had given Blaze to her. It seemed like fate that she was here. Her path was destined to connect with El Caballo Danza Magnifico. This place had been Blaze's home. Her special mare had grown up here. And now, Storm had brought Issie here too. It had to be more than a coincidence, didn't it? Issie put her hand up to touch the gold half-heart that hung around her neck. She knew at that moment that the Silver Bridle was not their only reason for coming here. She knew she had something else that she had to do.

As Roberto poured a second glass of sherry for each of them, Issie excused herself from the group. "I'm going down to the stables to check on the horses," she said.

The night air was warm against her skin as she walked across the cobbled courtyard in the dark to the stables. She entered the stallion stables and Angel poked his head out of the stall immediately to greet her with a friendly nicker.

The big grey horse had run so bravely for her in the

village square. He had been given a hero's welcome at the finish line – and he had relished it. As the wreath of red roses was strung around his neck in the ceremony afterwards, Angel had stood proud and noble, his head held high. He wore the scars of the *serreta* now as a badge of his courage, rather than a reminder of the cruelty that had once been inflicted on him. He was the champion of El Caballo. Their greatest horse. His race would be spoken of throughout the generations, would become part of the legend of the Silver Bridle in the time to come. Issie had always known he could do it, but as they'd crossed the finish line ahead of Vega even she'd had to admit she hadn't known the grey horse could run quite as fast as he did that day.

"You're a hero, Angel, you know that, don't you?" Issie whispered to the horse as she stroked his satin neck. "A real hero."

The stallion nickered to her and Issie pulled a carrot out of her pocket for him. "Even a hero likes a pony treat now and then," she giggled.

Further down the corridor, at the other end of the stallion loose boxes, Storm was also waiting for his carrot. He had his wee colt nose poking up over the Dutch door. He could hear Issie's voice down the corridor and he nickered anxiously, calling for the girl to come to see him. Then he bashed one of his front hooves impatiently against the door of his stall, insisting that she pay attention to him.

"Yeah, yeah, I know, I'm coming!" Issie called back to him, laughing at the colt's bolshy new attitude.

He had grown up so much even in the past few weeks. He was getting bigger now, he would be a yearling soon, and then what? Issie felt gripped with uncertainty. Sure, she knew a lot about horses, but did she really know how to train a young colt, how to school and prepare a horse with the amazing bloodlines and potential that Storm had? She remembered Roberto's offer. He had told her that he would school the colt, make him a true El Caballo stallion, in exchange for the colt's own progeny, his sons and daughters, when he grew up and became a stallion. Issie hadn't wanted to listen at the time. All she could think of was getting Storm back and taking him home with her, home to Winterflood Farm where Blaze and Comet were waiting.

But where was home? Could it be that the colt's home was here? At El Caballo Danza Magnifico? Here, he could run free each day in the green, sweet pastures of Andalusia with the mares and their colts. He could be schooled, as Blaze had been, in the classical style of the *haute école*. He could be given everything that she could not give him back in Chevalier Point.

Issie unbolted the door of Storm's stall and walked inside. The colt stood perfectly still as she ran a hand over his soft bay coat. He knew this girl, he trusted her touch. She would never hurt him, never betray him.

"You know," Issie said, feeling the tears already rolling down her cheeks as she realised what she had to do, "you know I love you, don't you, Storm? I came here to get you back. I love you more than anything. But I think this is what I have to do."

"Isadora?" There was a sound outside the stall now and Issie looked up and saw Francoise standing there. "Isadora?" Francoise saw the tears running down Issie's cheeks. "What is the matter, what's wrong?"

Issie couldn't speak at first. She felt as if she was ripping her own heart out doing this. She knew, though, that it was the right thing to do. She had to do it for Storm.

With trembling hands, she reached around the back of her neck and undid the clasp of the gold necklace.

The necklace fell into the palm of her hand and she gripped the chain with the broken heart tightly in her balled fist. She couldn't bring herself to let go. Then she took a deep breath, wiping the tears away with the back of her fist, and reached out her hand to Francoise.

"Here," she said, her voice shaking. She passed the necklace to Francoise.

The Frenchwoman recognised it immediately. "Isadora," she said, "this is the necklace that I gave to you. Half of a gold heart. The other half is attached to Blaze's halter."

Issie nodded. "I've never taken it off, Francoise. Since you gave it to me, I've always worn it as a symbol of my love. No matter where I am, half of my heart is always with Blaze."

She pressed the necklace firmly into Francoise's hand.

"When I leave, Francoise, will you do something for me? Will you take this half of the heart and put it on Storm's halter? I want him to know, I want him to know…" Issie had to stop speaking for a moment as the tears overwhelmed her, and then she continued. "I want Storm to know that half of my heart now will always be here at El Caballo with him."

"You are leaving him here? In Spain?" Francoise said.

Issie nodded. "I have to, Francoise. I don't want to, but I have to. I know that now. You'll look after him for me, won't you? And it won't be forever, will it?"

Francoise nodded. "I will look after him, of course.

He is in good hands here. It is a very great thing that you are doing, a brave thing also."

"Don't!" Issie said. "I don't want to think about it or I will change my mind."

And with that she threw her arms around the colt's neck and embraced him for what she knew would be the last time in a long while.

"I have to go now, Storm," she said slowly, reluctantly letting go of him. "Francoise will look after you now."

She put her hand on her chest where the necklace had once been. "I don't need the necklace. You'll be right here, in my heart with me always," she said, biting her lip now to stop the tears. "And I'll come back for you," she told him. "One day. I'll be back. That's a promise."